DARK MYSTERIES OF FATE

Tiffany Hepworth

ALSO BY TIFFANY HEPWORTH

Betrayal Kills

Play or Die

COMING SOON

A Fate Worse than Death

The Ruby, the Lady and the Killer

Regina Willow's Grave

ACKNOWLEDGMENTS

"I would like to say a massive thank you to my beta readers, alpha readers, ARC readers, my editor, my family and friends and everyone that has helped this book to progress with your supportive feedback, thank you.

A special thanks goes out to Maria Taylor, Israr Kakar, PL Waites, Mohammed Momoh, Teddy Oguntayo, Heather Cook, and Donna Taylor for your endless support for this book and everything in my life.

And finally, the biggest thank you to my amazing fiancé, Daniel Cook for reading every tweak of this book, giving valuable advice and believing in me always. You are my biggest supporter and I appreciate everything you do.

Prologue

Fate will always be a mystery. It is rumoured that it controls every aspect of our lives. Even that there is a path for every decision we make. Every mistake has a purpose. We all have an inevitable destiny that we cannot escape, no matter what we do. From the moment you are born, fate has a clear path carved for you and every little moment builds up to your death. We can struggle, we can squirm, we can scream. It all changes nothing. You can try to escape its grasp, but it will find you again.

Sometimes, there is the illusion that we have changed our fate, but we are wrong. Maybe the change you make to avoid your fate was supposed to happen anyway and you escaped nothing. The next time you put an occurrence down to a simple coincidence, think again. When you keep bumping into the same person over and over and still avoid them, think again. When you keep trying to force something to go your way, but it never works out, think again. When you're upset that something in your life changes or ends, think again. Your destiny is already set in stone and whatever is set in stone must never be removed.

Always remember, what will be will be.

STORY 1
RIDGEBROOKE

Chapter 1

It was time to face my worst nightmare. I couldn't hide from it any longer. As I stared past my dirty window wipers, I managed to see the road. I noticed the storm drawing in closer. The clouds were hanging miserably over my Ford Fiesta. I gazed up at the grey cloud, which looked as though it was going to weep heavily and drown me. I stopped looking at the stormy sky when I realised that I was swerving all over the road by turning the wheel too much to one side. *Come on Scarlet, concentrate,* I told myself over and over.

The last thing I wanted was a repeat of last year when I took my eyes off the road for barely a second but found myself crashing into a tree. I was lucky that I only broke my leg. I just had to tell myself that I was almost there. The village of Sandy Ville wasn't far away. All I wanted was for my mother to know that I didn't hate her during her final days. I still couldn't believe that she was on her death bed at just 46 years old, I thought I would have had longer to sort things. But your past has a way of creeping up on you. I couldn't let her pass away, thinking that the bad arguments we had in the past were still how I thought of her.

My phone began to vibrate. I looked down at it anxiously, hoping that it was not my brother Andrew telling me that I was too late. I reached over to press the green button on my phone screen, and I heard a loud screech. When I looked up from my phone, it seemed that I could no longer see the road. All that was in my vision was thick fog and dark mist. I slammed my brakes on and climbed out of the car with my phone still in my hand.

'Hello? Andrew is that you?' I yelled down the phone. He could probably hear panic forming in my voice.

'Yes, Scarlet, where are you? The doctor says she only has a few hours left. Are you close? Mum really wants to say her piece to you before it's too late,' Andrew said. I heard in his tone that he was finding all of this a lot harder than I was. In all the years I had known him, he hardly ever left her side.

'I am trying, but the storm is right on top of me. It just started lightening, and now I can't even see the road, only fog,' I explained to him as he sighed down my ear.

The grey cloud finally caved in and began to pour piercing cold rain onto the land around me. It pelted off the ground, and the smell of petrichor took over my senses. I took a look behind me and noticed that my car was suddenly not where I left it. I searched for the "2 miles to Sandy Ville" sign, but that was absent as well. *How could a sign and my car just disappear despite me leaving my car not one minute ago?*

'Something isn't right here, Andrew. I'm just two miles away from Sandy Ville, but my car is not where I left it. Oh, wait, I think I can see a village near me. Maybe I can go and find some help from someone.

Surely there is an explanation for this,' I said to my brother.

I felt my clothes become drenched in seconds. They began to weigh me down and drag helplessly on the floor behind me. I found that my feet began to lift off the ground faster the more I thought about being stuck out in a cold storm for much longer.

'That's strange. There is nothing but empty countryside from where you live to Sandy Ville. There should be no other villages. But just try and get help and get here soon. It's already 9 o 'clock and dark. Don't make me worry about you too. See you later sis,' Andrew said caringly.

'I'll try to be quick. There has to be some explanation for this, speak soon.' I put the phone down and began to walk further away from where I thought my car was.

I put my phone in my pocket and took a deep breath. There was always something about darkness and fog that frightened me. Perhaps it was because as a child, I had vivid nightmares about being chased by a killer in a foggy wood. Strange. I began to walk closer to the village that seemed to be just down the path. I squinted and tried to see through the thick fog. I couldn't see anything but the faint outlines of small buildings. I felt the mist break and brush my face and then reform as it moved past me.

I soon came to a sign that said 'Ridgebrooke'. *Where was I?* Surely, I hadn't travelled to a village I had never heard of on the way to my dying mother. My brother travelled a lot more than me and even he had never heard of a village in between my house and Sandy Ville. What was going on here? *Had I found an old, abandoned village?*

Despite not knowing how I got there, I continued to drag myself through the stormy weather to find help. I needed someone to help me find my car or at least explain how it could have disappeared out of sight. I walked up to the first building that I saw. It was old in style, but the lights were on, so I knew someone was in there.

The building had a big sign on the front saying 'Ridgebrooke Motel', so I entered curiously. The sign was made of antique grey wood, which made me wonder how old this place was and if it was really open for business. The letters looked ancient, as though they had been carved into the wood by hand.

I walked up to the old lady sitting at the desk reading a newspaper. I smiled at her gracefully and hoped for the best. It turned out that it was still open to the public. Maybe it was just an old building.

'Hello? I need some help. I was thrown off balance by the storm, and I somehow managed to lose my car. I tried to look for it, but I couldn't see through all of the fog. Have you got someone that could help me?' I asked.

The old lady slid her glasses down her nose and placed the paper down. I noticed her observing how I looked, but I said nothing.

'We don't get many outsiders visiting anymore. They say we are off the map. I can't get anyone to help you right now, as it's late, but I can offer you a room at half price for the night. You'll be able to look for your car in the morning once the storm is over. It's too dangerous to go back out there,' she said in a non-friendly voice. I tried to shake her unkindness off.

'I would usually stay over at such a late time with a storm, but I'm afraid I need help now. My mother is living her final hours you see, and I need to get to her before it's too late. Staying overnight would mean that I cannot say my final goodbye,' I expressed. I stared down at the floor and waited for tears to come, but they didn't show.

'Oh. I am sorry, but it's not negotiable. Whether your mother is dying or not, letting you go back out there would—well, it would complicate things even further. No, you must stay, I insist. But there is one condition,' the old lady said with a cunning smirk on her face.

I watched her mouth dribble on one side. I noticed her eye twitch and her freckles stretch on her face. I shuddered and tried to concentrate on why I was there in the first place. *Why couldn't she get someone to help me?*

'Sorry, that must have seemed quite demanding. What I meant to say was that I don't have anybody available at the moment. But I will in the next few hours. If you could just stay in a motel room until then? Dry off, relax, and then my caretaker Jimmy will help you,' she said.

It was something that I just had to accept. I could have tried somewhere else in the small village, but I couldn't get any better than a motel at half price. I did have some comfort knowing that within a few hours, I would get help. I hoped that by then, the storm would have calmed down. But I remembered what she said before. 'One condition.' *What did she mean by that?*

'Okay. I will stay for a little while, but I really must get back soon. But what did you mean earlier by "one condition?"' I asked nervously.

'Yes. If you die here, you must be buried here. That is the only condition for anyone staying in Ridgebrooke,' the old lady continued.

I froze. I felt my spine turn cold. I felt the blood in my veins turn to ice. *Why was a stranger who I thought wanted to help me suggesting that I could die here in just a few hours?*

Chapter 2

I happened to look up at the clock ticking away on the wall behind her. *How long had she been waiting for a response? What was I to say to such a question?* I opened my mouth and hoped that words of wisdom would come flowing out.

'Sorry if I am missing something here, but why would I die here? I am not moving here permanently or anything. I just need to stay for a few hours until my car can be found,' I insisted.

An eerie smile broke from her cheekbones and spread towards her bitter eyes. She tapped on her watch as though she was on borrowed time.

'Only a few hours, of course. Now, let me show you where you can wait,' she replied to me. *Is she purposely avoiding the question?*

She rushed out from behind the reception desk and showed me out of the door. I then followed her out of her tiny office and down the row of motel rooms. From the outside, they all seemed small and rough, but I could not ask for more for half price. The paint work was wearing and the front doors to the motel rooms were full of scratches.

I could tell that no maintenance had been done here for years, so why did she employ a caretaker? I kept my questions to myself to avoid offending her. She was already being generous by letting me stay here until she could help me.

'Here we are. Room eighteen. If anyone bothers you, just ignore them. I'm Brenda, by the way,' she said as she passed me the key with the number eighteen on.

She soon rushed off back to her office. I put my hand above my head in an attempt to stop the storm from soaking my clothes even further, but it was no use. I quickly turned the key in the door and ushered inside for shelter. I took a glance around the motel room. It was modest in size. It had a tiny single bed with mustard-coloured bedding. The walls were dark green, and the carpet was dirt brown.

I did not approve of Brenda's taste in furnishings, but I wasn't there to judge. But it did have a certain smell about it, like when you go up to an attic in an old, abandoned house. There was a strong smell of dust lingering in the air as though it hadn't been cleaned in decades.

I took it upon myself to get dry and rest before the caretaker came and helped me. I took my phone from my pocket to update my brother on my whereabouts. I was surprised to notice that the screen was smashed. I gasped and threw it down onto the bed. *How did it manage to break in my pocket?* I kept pressing the power button, hoping to see a sign of life, but the phone didn't respond. I was here alone. I couldn't help but fear that my mother's passing would arrive before I got to her home, and now, I had no way of staying updated.

I sighed and sat at the end of the bed. The mattress was sharp and uncomfortable, like a thousand pins poking me at once. I was alone in a strange town during a storm with no connection to the outside world. Surely, I was overthinking it and being paranoid. I would be out of here soon. I looked out of the tiny window and noticed the rain clattering against the window and bouncing off. Every so often, I saw a big flash of lightning shine through the skinny window blinds. What was I to do? I didn't want to just sit and wait for hours alone in my motel room.

I walked to the window to listen to the heavy rain. I stripped my top layer of clothing and laid them neatly by the fireplace to dry off. It was then that I noticed something impossible. *My car was outside my window.* It was definitely mine, as it was my number plate, but what had happened to it? It was covered in dust. I had only just had it washed. But how? Nobody said they had found it and brought it back, and it wasn't there when I came into room eighteen. I had to find out how it got there. I rushed out of the motel room and dashed back up to the office. It had an old, closed sign on the door, and it was full of cobwebs. I stopped and observed the sight before my eyes.

'Brenda? Hello, are you there?' I said with a slight stutter in my voice.

I then felt a sharp tap on my shoulder. I gasped and turned around quickly.

'What are you doing here, miss? This is not your property,' a police officer said to me. He held his police hat under one arm and a notebook in the other.

'Oh, hello, officer. The motel owner Brenda was letting me stay in room eighteen. My car went missing, you see, and she was kind enough to let me stay here until it was found,' I explained nervously.

I wondered why an officer would be interested in me staying in a motel room for a few hours.

'Brenda? The owner of this motel? She's been dead for the past twenty years, and this is now state property, and you are trespassing,' the officer said.

I froze and felt my voice box wobble and almost shatter into pieces. It was impossible; it had to be. The woman had just given me a room, of course she was alive. I began to laugh and hoped that he was joking.

'There must be a mistake? I was waiting for the caretaker to find my car, but it suddenly appeared on the driveway,' I told him. I could see the disbelief in his eyes.

'Nope. No mistake. This place has been closed for twenty years since the owner, Brenda, died. Please, let me take you somewhere else, I insist,' the officer stated.

I felt a pit of nerves in my stomach like a mountain of worms moving around but I managed to drag myself to the car. I tried to think about what he told me, but his words didn't sink in. He opened the police car door for me as the rain stopped me in my tracks. I was soaked through in just a few seconds. She *couldn't* be dead. *Could she?*

Chapter 3

Before I had the chance to consider Brenda not being alive, my eyes forced themselves open, and my lungs filled with dusty air as I breathed rapidly. I scanned my environment and saw the mustard-coloured bedding that I found myself laid upon. I was definitely in room eighteen of the motel. I thought of nothing but Brenda. *Was the incident with the cop just a dream?* I looked over at the clothes by the fire that looked almost dry, only a few crinkles showing. I walked to the other side of the motel room and threw the clothes on. I then headed over to the door and turned the knob. It wouldn't open. *I had been locked in.*

'Hello? Excuse me! Brenda? I've been, erm, locked in!' I kept banging on the door, hoping someone passing would hear. Then I continued, 'Is anyone there? Hello!' I felt my breath getting faster, and my legs began to shake. I could feel nothing but panic. I then heard footsteps. I heard the lock turning, and the door flew open.

'Scarlet? What was all that yelling?' Brenda said as she stared up at me. I was a lot taller than her.

I couldn't help but sigh with relief. All I could think about was being locked in the motel room forever.

'Why was my room locked? And how did my car end up outside?' I explained in a rush. My words tumbled over each other.

Brenda glared at me with confusion but also distress. She looked behind her as though she was making sure nobody else was around.

'Why so many questions! You young people do worry too much. You will die young if you are not careful. Your head will explode, and your guts will fail and fall out,' Brenda said viciously.

I gasped and almost lost my balance. I reached over and grabbed the worn-out armchair by the motel room door.

'How incredibly … gory of you to say. I will try not to worry that much. Just please explain what is going on here,' I said, lowering my voice and taking deep breaths.

She began to laugh at my distress. I found it very unnerving.

'There are some things that you just don't need to know about! The caretaker tried to find your car all night, it's outside my office. So, your car being outside your room must have been a dream. I came in to check on you, but you were fast asleep, so I didn't bother waking you. We locked all the motel doors because the storm was bad. With the doors being so old and worn, they bang a lot with bad wind. See? Nothing to worry about!' Brenda explained with a sickening smile on her face. Brenda turned around and went to walk back to her office. I took a quick glance out of the window, but my rusty-looking car was nowhere to be seen. *It couldn't have been moved if it was in such a state.*

'And the officer?' I asked. I folded my arms and waited to see what she would come up with this time.

She stopped in her tracks and turned back around to face me. Her eyes suddenly bloodshot and her face paler than before.

'Officer? What are you talking about darling?' She asked, kindly but coldly.

She began to hold her hands tightly together and twiddle her thumbs. I looked down and noticed her toes wiggling. She was fidgeting, which meant she was hiding something, *surely.*

'The officer last night? He said I was trespassing by being here. He also said that you died twenty years ago, and this place has been shut ever since,' I explained. My voice began to stutter when she glared at me evilly as I spoke.

'What nonsense! There was no officer here last night. And as you can tell, I am still alive and well. You must have been dreaming. Now, if you don't mind, I have a motel to run. Since I let you stay here for half price last night, you can leave now,' Brenda stated. She then hurried off and left me, so I couldn't ask any more questions.

She was acting cagey. I went back into the motel room and began to gather what little items I had with me. I put the motel money on the dressing table for her to collect when she went in. I felt reassured knowing my car was back outside, and I could finally go to my mum's house. I had no idea if she was even still alive, and since my phone was smashed, I had no way of finding out. My only hope was to drive there and hope for the best. I needed to get out of the strange motel and get my head together.

I grabbed my phone and headed to my car, which had been parked in the tiny parking lot of the motel by the caretaker. I didn't thank Brenda for letting me stay the night. I felt afraid when I was around her, so I didn't even bother to say goodbye. I hopped into my car and began to drive away from the motel. I was more than glad that the storm was over, and my car had been found. I hated how I couldn't ask the caretaker where he had found it.

I looked at the motel in my car mirror and watched it fade away into the distance. I felt my stomach begin to rumble badly. I realised that I hadn't eaten anything since the day before. I kept driving down the long main road of Ridgebrooke until I came to a traffic light stop. I looked around and noticed a small snack shop on the corner to my left. I put my indicator on and drove into the tiny car park. I felt nothing but relief to be away from that creepy old motel and to be somewhere modern and normal. *Or so I thought.*

The outside of the snack shop was painted a light yellow with the sign 'snack and go' just above the door in neon green letters. I heard a loud bell ring just above my head as I entered. The inside of the shop shocked me. It was not modern or tasteful like the outside. There were cobwebs hanging from the ceiling. Mainly just dust on the shelves and the floor was full of dirt. The walls had plaster coming away from it, and the curtains were a dark lime green full of muck. I tried to hide the judgement from my face, but it shone through.

'Yes, miss, can I help you?' an old, croaky voice said from behind the counter.

I soon stopped looking and judging. I spun around to face him. I painted a fake smile onto my face to avoid suspicion.

'Oh hello. I am not from around here as you probably guessed. I stayed in the motel last night because of the storm, but now I'm heading out of town. I'm starving, so I wanted to grab some snacks for the road. But ... I can't seem to find anything,' I explained.

I observed him. He was in his mid-70s, with short grey hair and stubborn looking. He had one fake eye that couldn't look anywhere but the floor and a big scar down the side of his left cheek. He was dressed as an old-fashioned farmer with a chequered shirt and dungarees. *Unusual for a shop owner.*

'As you can see, I don't have a lot of stock left. I am shutting down and retiring, hence the bare shelves. I can see what I have in the back?' He said. I felt grateful for his efforts.

'Thank you. That would be so kind. I would go somewhere else, but I've never been to this town before,' I said. He then went into the storeroom behind his till. I heard him mutter a reply as he walked off, something like 'no, nobody has ever been here before.' *What could he mean by that?*

I continued to observe the shop as he was busy trying to find me some snacks in the back. *Why was everywhere around here so old and on the brink of shutting down?* I kept walking around. I felt the bottom of my shoes clinging to the dust and mud all over the floor. There was no carpet or wood. It was concrete. The shop hadn't seen a lick of paint or any refurbishment within the last forty years at least. It seemed that the whole town was falling apart.

I stopped searching when a shiny gold reflection caught my eye. It reflected in the glass of a tiny window. I followed the shine to the desk near the till. Then I saw it. A large Victorian pocket watch in perfect condition. *He can clean his pocket watch but not his shop? It was precious to him.* I took it into my hands gently and opened the catch. I stared down at the meticulous and gorgeous watch that fascinated me a lot more than I originally thought it would.

'What are you doing? Put that down AT ONCE!' I heard the man yell from the doorway of the storeroom. He held a small box of snacks in his hands.

I grabbed onto the pocket watch and held it tight as I imagined it slipping out of my hands and smashing into tiny pieces on the ground below me. I put it back where I found it immediately.

'I am sorry, sir. I noticed it shining, and I, well, I just had to take a closer look,' I explained trying to sound reasonable. I suddenly felt like a scalded schoolgirl again.

'You should never mess with time! That there holds the whole universe and those that are not residents of Ridgebrooke should never handle it! Give it back to me now!' the man yelled. He reached over and snatched the pocket watch from the counter.

I stared at his glass eye, which looked as though it was about to shatter with any more shouting. He quickly placed the pocket watch into his pocket. He then slammed a small box down onto the counter.

'Here, take your goods and leave me alone! I don't even want your money, just go!' he gasped.

I quickly threw my arms around the box and dashed out of the shop. I had a quick glance into the box. It had crisps, chocolate bars, and a few almost out-of-date packet sandwiches. I loaded my free goods into the car and went to get in, but the shop owner rushed out after me.

'Oh, and by the way, you are wanted at the Ridgebrooke Cemetery. They like visitors there…' he said to me from the doorway. His look of anger had vanished. He had a proud and evil smirk upon his face as he spoke. I stood by my car with the keys in my hand, trying to make sense of his words. *Why would I need to go to the cemetery?*

Chapter 4

I had been following the odd signs on the road that said 'Ridgebrooke Cemetery'. I didn't understand why I was needed in the cemetery. *Who would need me other than Brenda?* Perhaps I didn't give her the right amount of money for the motel room. *No.* That couldn't be right. She would just meet me at the motel, not the cemetery. I kept driving along the uneven, bumpy road until I came to a sign that had a gravestone and a left arrow. I pulled in and parked my car by the gates on a tiny patch of grass.

I began to approach the almost filled cemetery. There were hardly any spaces left for any more bodies, it seemed almost full. I felt the cold wind strike my face like a sharp pointy icicle. Even though it was just after 10 a.m., there was a mysterious mist in the air like a suffocating puff of black smoke. I walked the length of one side of the cemetery, but I didn't see a soul until I finally saw someone out of the corner of my eye. I turned around quickly and noticed a young woman sitting on the bench. *She was not there before. I was almost certain that I was alone when I arrived.*

She had golden ginger locks of hair that flew wildly past her shoulders. Her eyes were the colour of grass, and her skin was as pale as a gleaming cloud. She was wearing a knee length skirt with small flowers on it. She had a plain blue top tucked into her skirt. *Was she ordinary?*

'Excuse me? I am supposed to be meeting someone here, but I can't see anyone?' I asked timidly. I didn't dare to step any closer to the mysterious young woman.

'I don't know anything about that. Sorry,' she replied. Her voice was soft and low.

I nodded my head and continued to walk down the winding path of the cemetery, searching for answers. I looked back and saw the woman gazing at me sadly. Her eyes were pools of misty water poisoned with misery. Some of the gravestones looked hundreds of years old. *Where were the newer graves?* I heard the leaves crunching under my worn shoes and the wind slowly blowing in my ear.

'You'd better leave,' I heard the young woman say.

I turned around and looked back at her. My mother had always told me to look at people when I spoke to them. Her motherly influence was still shadowing me. She was still anxiously waiting on the bench. I stopped walking on the path and faced her.

'Leave? But I have only just come here? I am supposed to be meeting someone,' I said with nothing but confusion overriding my whole face.

'The rain is coming. You don't have long,' she said. Her voice began to shake as she spoke.

'Sorry?' I asked. *It rained a lot here. But why was she warning me about the rain?*

I heard the clattering of thunder above me. It suffocated my ear drums and made my skin prickle with goosebumps. I was in the middle of the cemetery, and I had nowhere to turn to for shelter this time. *I guess I would just have to go back to my car.* I began to pace towards my car before the heavy rainfall crashed upon me. Just seconds later, the sky turned almost black. *But it was morning?* I concentrated on getting to my car to avoid being drenched again. After all, I had no change of clothes, and the rain was beyond freezing last time.

Once the sky was blackened by dark grey clouds all around me, the rain began to pour more heavily. There was never light drizzle here, only ice-cold pelting rain like hailstone made of pins. I continued to trot down the winding path of the cemetery until I got to where I had parked my car. *Where was it? It was definitely here when I parked it.*

I then felt a slight vibration in my pocket. I reached in and grabbed my phone. I stared at it with disbelief. *The screen wasn't cracked, and it was working perfectly fine.* I had a text from my boss that said, 'Your week holiday is confirmed. Have a nice time!' I stared at the text message. *Having a week off from being a private investigator was great ... if I didn't take it off to say goodbye to my dying mother.*

I stood near the entrance of the cemetery, holding a phone that was broken last night, wondering how it happened. I could hardly see the screen as the rain drops covered it. Within about two minutes, my hair was soaked through, and my clothes began to feel incredibly heavy. I almost dropped my phone when I noticed the date at the top of the screen.

Wednesday 13th April 2022. *What? But that was ... yesterday? I had to make sense of this.* I left my house at 3 p.m. on the 13th of April for Sandy Ville when I got stuck in traffic and got hit by the storm. I then slept in a motel room overnight until the storm settled, so today *had* to be the 14th of April.

In fact, I *knew* it was because when I drove in my car this morning on the way to the snack shop, my dashboard said the 14th of April. I went onto the map on my phone to figure out exactly how to get out of this village, which seemed never-ending. I typed in Ridgebrooke and set it as my current location. *No match found. What was happening? How was any of this possible? I needed to find my car and just keep driving until I got out of this town.* I marched quickly in the rain. I dragged myself with every step, and I exited the cemetery. As I walked out, I saw a car zooming on the road in front of me.

Wait, is that my number plate?

'Hey! You! Stop!' I yelled as I tried to run after the car.

My car had been stolen! Could the trip to this town get any worse? I stopped running after my car a few seconds after I started. My lungs weighed me down and felt as though they were about to puncture. *I had to report my car stolen, or I would be stuck here for longer.*

I went up to the old sign by the road and tried to look at it through the heavy rain. There were many signs pointing in different directions. I could only just make out what they said. It looked like they had been there for centuries. I saw the police department sign and began to head that way. *Why were there never many cars on this main road? It's funny how I've never gone past this village before when I used to go to Sandy Ville a lot.*

I texted my brother before I lost signal. I told him that I was stranded in a town called Ridgebrooke and that I needed help. *Surely it wouldn't be long before he came out here for me.* Luckily, it wasn't a long walk from the cemetery to the police station. *Finally, some good luck.* I dragged myself in through the double blue doors, and I was delighted to see an officer sitting behind the desk.

'Hello officer? I would like to report my car stolen,' I insisted. I rested my arms on the front desk.

The officer had a round physique and shocking blue eyes. His uniform looked messy and out of place. He looked as though he hadn't shaved in weeks.

'Okay, miss. Name and registration plate, please?' he asked miserably. Nobody broke a smile around here.

'It's Scarlet Carlson. My reg is AF68 WX0,' I said enthusiastically. *My car surely couldn't have gone far by now.*

He began to type on his computer.

'You are in luck. That car has just gone past our security cameras outside. They were going a bit fast, so it registered on our cameras. Here, take a look,' the officer said.

He turned his CCTV camera screen towards me so I could see for myself. *That was definitely my car.*

'Wait? Is this a wind up, Miss Carlson? Because we don't have time for games,' the officer told me.

'What? No. My car zoomed past me about ten minutes ago. I need it to get home, so I came here to report it missing,' I explained agitatedly.

'Then please explain why you are the one on our security cameras, driving your own car not five minutes ago?' he said.

He then zoomed in to a security camera from outside the cemetery. *The whole town had security cameras.* It showed me waving and chasing after my own car. But when he zoomed in, the person driving my car was wearing *my clothes* and looked *exactly* like me.

It was impossible.

Chapter 5

I kept looking at the camera footage, hoping there was a mistake. *Unless I had another twin that I didn't know about wearing the exact same clothes, then this definitely was impossible.* I kept taking small steps backwards until I found myself at the door of the station.

'I have to go. I am sorry that I bothered you,' I blurted out with a shaking voice.

I ran back through the double doors and didn't dare to look back. My mind completely disconnected from my surroundings; it was too much to take in. I found my breathing becoming rapid and out of control. I *needed* answers. *But how?* All I could think to do was retrace my steps. I began to jog back to the cemetery. The pouring rain was turning into a drizzle.

I could see a glimpse of sunshine shining through the catastrophic clouds that dangled over me. I soon found myself back at the cemetery. I thought through everything.

I was standing here, then the woman warned me about the rain. How could she tell it was coming if I couldn't? Then I got drenched by the rain, then my car went missing, and then my broken phone was suddenly not broken. And after that, I realised the date was wrong on my phone. I saw my car driving down the road, so I went to the station to report it stolen. But still, none of it makes sense. Then the rain cleared. It had been raining for about fifteen minutes, much less than before. I stood and stared down at my soaking clothes.

I reached into my pocket to check if my phone was still working. When I looked at it, *the screen was cracked again.* I moved my eyes to where I parked my car before it went missing. *It had returned. But it had been stolen. What was happening here?*

'If you repent your sins, all will be well!' I heard a loud male voice yell from behind me.

'My sins? Excuse me?' I asked. *He was not there before either.*

He was standing near the small village church. I observed him closely. He was holding a sign that said, 'find the lord', next to a small wooden table that had leaflets.

'Will you join my campaign, miss? This small village has seen enough evil! It is time to find the Lord and repent!' the man said.

He was tall with long grey hair to his shoulders, although he was going bald at the front. His eyes were perfectly circular and almost black. He was wearing a long black gown with a clerical collar on it. *Did priests usually try to convert people to a specific religion in a cemetery?*

'I am sorry, but I am not religious. And I can't sign up to the church here. I am not from Ridgebrooke, I am trying to go to Sandy Ville,' I explained.

I smiled awkwardly at the priest, and I tried to walk away, but he spoke again and distracted me.

'You might be here a lot longer than you anticipated, Scarlet. What a lovely name! Scarlet red, *blood* red. I would repent while you have the time. Time is *everything* in this village,' the priest said. In a certain light, his eyes looked bloodshot red.

I wiped the tiny raindrops from my forehead and tried to figure out why a priest was doing his campaign in a cemetery outside a small church that looked as though it hadn't been open to the public in years.

'Time is everything here? What are you trying to say? Look, I can't stand and chat. I've been here for too long. My car is just over there. I need to get in it and drive far away from here as soon as possible,' I said in an authoritative tone.

'And what about your mother? Do you think she will wait until you get there to drift away into a forever sleep? Or will she be something else that weighs down your conscience?' the priest said.

I froze unexpectedly. It felt as though my whole body had suddenly forgotten how to function. I felt a terrifying shock run through my muscles; it almost made me shudder at the sound of his words. I wanted to fall to the floor and give up trying to leave Ridgebrooke, but I somehow found the strength to keep composure. I took a deep breath and faced him once again.

'How did you know my name and how do you know about my dying mother? What is with this place! It feels like everyone knows my secrets, and they are taunting me with them!' I exclaimed. My body had maintained its composure, but my voice was beginning to crack and break and become fragile like an outdated musical instrument that had been destroyed. He then pointed to the graves around us.

'You need to remember to watch your tone, just as the dead are currently watching you. How I know these things is not the concern here. It is what you are going to do that matters,' he said calmly with his hands entwined.

'Please stop speaking in riddles! I have had it with this town! I don't know you or anyone else here, so I am taking my leave. I was in a bad storm and then I lost my car so I—' I tried to explain, but I was interrupted.

'You then went to the motel to seek help in finding your car. You stayed in the motel for the night. By the morning, your car appeared, but you had no explanation why. You came here today, and another storm came that made you go back to yesterday. Then you chased your own car. Yes?' He retold what had happened in the exact right way.

I glared at him viciously. My eyes were slowly sinking towards the muddy ground. My lips were slowly parting with shock. I felt the fresh air that I kept breathing in suddenly drain from my lungs bit by bit.

'How … how could you possibly know all this? You better start explaining, or I'll—' I said, but he interrupted once again.

'You will what? There is no use in me explaining. You need to figure this out for yourself. One chance. That is all you have,' he said.

I tried to figure out the riddles that he was speaking in. *What had all these strange events been leading up to?* I went to walk away and go to my car, but I felt the ground shake underneath me. *What was happening now?* I looked at the priest for help, but he took a step back. All he did was point to the grave that I was standing next to. It caught my attention. It said, 'Scarlet Carlson, 1988-2022.'

'No!' I screamed.

The mud below me caved in. It felt like quicksand, forcing me deeper underground. I could smell the mud and earth that surrounded me. There was nothing but darkness. I began to fall deeper. Could this really be the end?

Chapter 6

17 YEARS AGO

'Mother? Can I borrow some money? I have this school trip coming up and—' Andrew called out.

'Do you even need to ask my precious? You can have however much you need; I have always told you that. Anything for my special boy,' Mother replied to him.

I sighed, twiddling my loose hair around my finger. *Why was she so caring towards him? Maybe I should try being nice to her?*

'Actually, mother. I was going to ask if I could have a day off from chores this week? It's just I have been set an extra project to get my grades up and well

I—' I opened up, trying to be honest and hoping for reason.

'Excuses, excuses, excuses. That seems to be all that ever comes out of your mouth! You will do the chores! Do you think I don't have better things to do than clear up your mess? But I do it, every single day! Even in my condition! So, do as I say! I mean it, Scarlet. No man will want you if you cannot even keep on top of the housework!' She screamed. I was tired of her voice grating on my skin.

Just once I wanted her to listen to me, to treat me with kindness as she did with Andrew. Why did she not care about me?

'That's it, I've had it with this family! You can both go to hell!' I yelled.

I walked past them both and tossed the coffee table forcefully to one side as I stormed off. I didn't care if I ruined her perfectly expensive marble coffee table, she didn't deserve nice things if she was to treat her daughter like that. Perfect little Andrew got whatever he wanted; I wasn't allowed one little outburst. What did she expect if she was to treat me so poorly all the time? I looked back with a mischievous smirk on my face but what I saw was something that would haunt me forever. My mother, huddled over on the floor, holding her stomach and Andrew kneeling next to her.

'Are you okay mother? I will phone for an ambulance!' Andrew squeaked.

He ran to the phone and began to dial the number. I froze in my spot, staring through the living room doorway. Her eyes locked onto mine.

'You evil, evil witch! You will pay for this! You wished us to hell and here we are!' Her voice become vulnerable, soft. Something I had never witnessed before. *Surely nothing was wrong, it was only the small shove of a coffee table.*

But then I looked down and saw her beige woven carpet suddenly turn red. Blood was pouring from in between her legs and leaking onto the carpet.

Maybe she was right, we were in hell. I would burn for this.

NOW

I had been warned. My first night here, Brenda said if I stayed, then I had to die here. But not for one second did I believe it to be true. *Was this really it? Was I about to suffocate in a grave marked with my name?* I felt the mud and earth piling on top of me. I clawed away at my face to remove the dirt from my nostrils. *I had to keep breathing, I had to survive. Come on! You can get out of this!* I thought of everything the priest had said. It was clear that I was here for a reason, and I only had one chance to figure it out before the ground swallowed me up.

I felt myself continuously falling until I hit the bottom and bumped my head on the surface. I quickly rushed to my feet and looked around to get my bearings. It was dark, and I could only just make out where I was, but it looked like a tunnel. I did see a tiny dot of light to my left, which gave me hope. I had no idea why the ground gave way and made me fall into a grave with my name on it that led to a small tunnel. *Nothing in this town made sense, but I needed answers.*

I began to follow the small shining light, hoping it was the way out of the tunnel. Seeing my name upon a gravestone had put my whole life into perspective. I was already trying to come to terms with the impending death of my mother, but now I had to consider that I would also pass away this year. *Not knowing when or how was the worst part.* I thought I would at least reach middle age. I began to speed walk through the dark tunnel, searching for answers, but mostly for freedom. I had a million questions running through my mind at once, all fighting to be at the forefront of my thinking. *Why did a priest let me fall into a grave without rescuing me? How did he know things about my life?*

I doubt they were questions that would ever be answered truthfully. *If they were ever answered at all.* I stopped thinking and turned my head toward something that I had spotted. *Drawings and words.* They had been painted onto the side of the tunnel, but they were slowly fading off the hard muddy rocks. If they were not painted in bright white, I would not have been able to see them, as it was too dark to focus on anything but the light ahead. I stepped a little closer to observe what the paintings were showing me. As a trained private investigator, I always looked deeper into things to find the truth, and this situation would be no different.

There was the word "Ridgebrooke" painted high at the top of the wall in big bold letters. So, the drawing *had* to be something to do with the town. The first drawing showed a man walking alone near the Ridgebrooke sign. It said underneath the drawing 'lost.' I dared to move my eyes to the next drawing. It showed the same man cowering underneath a large umbrella and it said 'protection.' Then, on the next drawing, the man was staring down at a picture of a family, presumably his family. The word underneath that one said 'prevention.'

I began to wonder what these drawings meant. I then looked down to the final row of drawings, which had just two side by side. The first one showed the man trying to run out of the town, and it said 'denial.' The final one was of the man kneeling down and a priest impaling him in the chest with a religious cross. It had 'death' written underneath it.

I felt my legs trying to sink beneath me, but I remained standing. *What did the words lost, protection, prevention, denial, and death mean? And what did it have to do with this town?* I looked around for more clues but that is all the tunnel revealed. The drawings looked decades old, so they must have been relevant to this town for a very long time.

I headed towards the light at the end of the tunnel carrying a mental picture of the drawings with me. It was only a small tunnel, so I wondered where I would end up at the other end. I walked out of the tunnel after thinking that the ground collapsing would be the end of my life. I felt relieved to still be alive. When I got out of the tunnel, I looked around to see where I was. I was just outside of the cemetery.

'They have been there since the Middle Ages. It is sacred to us,' the priest said from behind me. He was still standing in the same position.

I wiped the mud from my hair and face and turned to him. I could not hide the bitterness from my expression.

'You watched me sink, and you were willing to let me die. What sort of priest are you! I don't care how long that tunnel has been there, it is not my concern!' I exclaimed.

'No, not the tunnel. The drawings. They have been there for as long as we can all remember. It shows the process,' the priest continued.

'What process?' I asked, trying to understand him.

'Well, people come to Ridgebrooke when they are *lost* on their way to somewhere else. Then they need *protection* from the rain to be safe. Then they think of what they have left behind and how they could have *prevented* whatever is about to happen. Then the panic comes. They try to get out of town as fast as they can when the *denial* sets in. But if things don't work out, they meet their *death* here instead,' he explained.

'Wait … so this happens to other people? Are you saying I'm stuck here forever until I die?' I asked in a panicked voice.

'If you haven't worked that out yet, then I cannot help you. In fact, I wasn't supposed to help you at all. I could see how much you are suffering, so I wanted to help you. I do help the ones I can, but I can only tell you what is to come if you repent your sins,' he said wickedly.

'Repent? What do I have to repent? I am no sinner!' I exclaimed. I just had a desperate need to get out of the town that continued to suffocate me, or it would drain the oxygen from my lungs and let me die silently.

'I'm afraid there is no use in denying things to me. I can see into your soul. Into everybody's souls. I know the things you have done. To your poor mother, your brother, old friends. You are not the person you seem to be,' he went on.

I felt his eyes all over me as though he was using his godly fire to burn through my skin and lure me further into the darkness.

'Okay, fine. I repent. I did some very bad things, and I regret them. Now, can I get out of here?' I begged, sounding almost too desperate.

'I do not know whether to believe you. But perhaps I should. The only thing I can tell you right now is that you are definitely due to die, and you need to be careful who you trust. But don't think that just because I know things that I can get you out of here because that's impossible. You have to find your own way out,' he answered.

I stared at him ferociously. I *needed* him to tell me. Did I want to know when and how I was going to die? *No.* But it was better to be prepared, that is the motto I always went by. I stood and waited to hear my fate.

'Your mother. She is still deeply angry with you. It has been years since you last saw her. Even during your childhood, the relationship was bad, was it not? Fighting, arguing. You were awfully cruel to her. You did things that she can never forgive you for, ever,' he began.

'And yet she wants me by her side when she drifts off into her deep sleep and never wakes up. That is where I was supposed to be now. But she may be dead already by the time I reach her. How exactly do you know all this?' I explained impatiently.

'And why do you think she wanted you there? That close to her? Your chest to her shoulder? Your right cheek upon her left cheek? Can you not think of any other reason other than to end you herself? As for how I know all this, you are the private investigator, work it out,' he told me as the weak mist around us grew thicker.

'End me? My mother is no killer! If I have been brought here because my mother is going to murder me on her deathbed, then … just no! I need to leave, she would never…' I said as I began to back away from the priest. *How did he know my occupation, my past, everything! No, I couldn't trust him!*

'Time is running out, Scarlet. Whether you believe me or not, your fate is in your hands. You can prevent your mother from killing you or find a way out of here and let it happen. But I did my part,' he said.

No, my mother, my own mother could never kill me! No matter how dark our past was, she could never murder her own child minutes before she perished herself! I began to run away from the graveyard towards the road, which was where the motel was. I *had* to get out of here, now more than ever.

I kept running and running until I felt my lungs almost squeeze themselves up through my windpipe and spill out of my mouth. I ran past the motel eventually. *I should be heading out of Ridgebrooke, the way I came.* I had given up trying to find my disappearing car. I had given up trying to rely on others to rescue me by way of a broken phone.

This was my life and only I had full control over it. I smiled to myself when I was out of breath, but I saw the "welcome to Ridgebrooke sign" fly past me as I ran. I was relieved to run past the sign finally. It felt like I had been trapped in the town for weeks. I kept running down the winding road where the storm first hit me, and then I *stopped.* Wait, what? I took a few seconds to process what my eyes were telling me.

I was back on the road just outside the graveyard. No! It couldn't be happening, it was impossible! The priest was nowhere to be seen. *There was nobody.* I began to run again. Perhaps I had taken a wrong turn? Yes! Maybe. I somehow found the physical endurance to run the whole way again.

I ran, and I ran, and I ran until I saw the snack shop, the motel, the Ridgebrooke sign. *I was definitely out of Ridgebrooke this time.* I felt the smile slowly creeping back onto my face. I stopped to finally take a breath now that I was safe. But as soon as I raised my head, *there was the graveyard.* How?! I felt my cheeks become flushed. I felt my heart strings almost snap. How did the road out of Ridgebrooke keep bringing me to the other side of Ridgebrooke, back where I had started?

I had to get out, there had to be a way! It was just a town after all. So, I ran. And I ran. I kept running, but I had only the same results over and over again. I ran until I couldn't run anymore, and I collapsed on the road outside of the cemetery. And then it dawned on me. *I really was trapped here.*

Chapter 7

THEN

'You don't understand! We need to find shelter. The rain is coming!' Lacey yelled to her long-term boyfriend.

'I cannot stand another moment in this strange town! How did a day of camping turn into this? I've never even heard of a town called Ridgebrooke!' Spencer called back to her.

He slammed his body down onto a bench that sat perfectly in the street, although chipped wood was all that was left of it. His girlfriend came and sat beside him with her arms folded.

'So, what is your plan? We just sit here and wait for the rain to fall again? I am not going back to 1976! We need to go before something weird happens again!' Lacey cried out.

'I keep telling you, we were not in 1976! That is impossible!' he replied. He made his beliefs very clear.

'You might think it is nonsense, but it's not! Why else would there be a calendar up in the police station saying 1976? All the decor was old as well!' she said. It was painful for her to not be believed by her love.

'Are you seriously saying that just because there was a thunderstorm during our camping trip, that we got thrown back into 1976 in a town that we have never heard of? Then when the rain stopped, we were randomly back in 2010? I don't think so! Have you thought that maybe the cops just don't change their calendar?' he declared with disbelief.

'I don't know how it happened, okay! I'm not a weather woman who has a time machine! I am just saying something's not right about this town! It was never on our map, and every time the rain comes, something happens. The clouds are darkening again now, so we need to leave the town before it happens again!' Lacey screeched, almost scratching her eyeballs out when he didn't listen to her words.

'Whatever. I have had enough of this! It is never just a nice weekend with you, is it? It always has to be full of drama. I have told you! Our best bet is to go back to the police station and tell them that we want our parents to pick us up because we are lost,' Spencer said lightly.

'And how do we explain getting lost in the forest near Sandy Ville? We will get the "You two are seventeen, you need to be more responsible" talk. They will never let us leave the house again! Your mother already thinks I'm bad for you!' Lacey squirmed.

Spencer sighed as loud as he could. His voice echoed and alarmed the birds of prey around them. He then dragged himself off the bench and began to walk out of town. But his intentions to escape the unknown town were put on pause as a cluster of distressed clouds began to group grimly above him. Their eerie grasp was too suffocating to escape from. He felt the trickles of rain drizzle down the back of his neck. Lacey looked above her at the narrowing blue skies and the growing ashen clouds. She rushed over to Spencer and tried tugging at his jacket.

'I am serious! We need shelter! The rain will come down on us before we even make it out of the town!' Lacey yelled. Her voice vibrated violently in the surrounding hell of cries. She yanked at his arm with anguish. He finally saw the torture in her eyes.

'Fine. If it really bothers you that much, then we will go somewhere. But where? I doubt anyone in this town will be welcoming to two outsiders,' Spencer expressed in a monotone voice of hopelessness.

Lacey began to walk in the opposite direction, and her boyfriend followed. She pelted down the narrow path that led to a short cut to the snack shop. She nervously dragged her boyfriend inside. They made it in with only a few drops of rain on them.

'There, we will be safe here. As soon as the showers have passed, we can go home,' a self-assured Lacey announced. Spencer smiled with agreement.

'Back again?' an old, croaky voice said from behind the counter.

'Oh, hello again, erm, sir. We just came in here for shelter. We will be gone soon,' Spencer quickly answered.

'You cannot escape it forever. It is your destiny to be caught in that rain or else you would not be here,' the man said while cleaning the counter vigorously.

'Sorry, what does that mean exactly?' a nervous Lacey replied.

The old shop owner grabbed his worn metal walking stick from behind the counter and began to wobble towards them, constantly leaning on his walking stick for support.

'When you planned to go camping, you were supposed to camp at the Sandy Ville Camping Ground, correct?' the old man said.

The young couple glared at each other with uncontrollable despair. The shop owner was happy to drown in their fear.

'Yes … that is right. But on our way to Sandy Ville, our car just stopped working so we had to camp just outside of Sandy Ville. We didn't realise it was Ridgebrooke at first. But—' Spencer told him, but he was abruptly interrupted.

'But then the rain came? And you found yourselves in a state of confusion and fear? Now you are trying to escape Ridgebrooke and make it home unharmed?' he asked. Just the sound of his unearthly voice was enough to make the teenagers quake.

'Erm … yes. Sorry, how do you know all this? It's just since we got here, we haven't told a soul. We haven't seen anyone apart from you earlier when we bought a drink. We are exhausted, and we just need to get home. We have no idea how long we have been here or anything, we just—' he was interrupted again. His girlfriend stood as still as a haunted cursed statue beside him, one that wanted to desperately break free but found herself stuck in fate's vicious hands.

'You have been here for thirty-five days. And that time will keep increasing the more you deny what is truly happening here. I wouldn't normally help the wanderers of Ridgebrooke, but you two are the youngest I have seen here. I used to be a father myself, and I do not want any harm to come to the youth. It is much too early for you two to—' the man said before he stopped in his tracks.

Lacey and Spencer darted their eyes around the snack shop and looked at each other with sharpened pupils and fresh fear.

'Too early for us to … what?' Lacey asked. Her voice screeched like long yellow fingernails running down a blackboard as she tried to hold in the tears that would eventually break through her eyeballs and scatter down her face.

'To perish,' he said quietly. His voice was overpowered by the sound of the hammering thunder that grappled over the building. Spencer held his companion close as the thunder caught them both off guard.

The silence felt as though it would make their ears bleed.

'You have been here a long time. The more it rains, the less time you have. You need to figure things out because it can only ever end in one of two ways,' the man said, his voice weakening towards the end of his sentence.

'Two ways? What are those?' Spencer asked, huddling his girlfriend into his arms tightly.

'You either acknowledge your sins and forgive yourself for them and face whatever is back home waiting for you. Or you continue to live in denial here and live here for the rest of your days. No leaving, you will be trapped here forever. So many of us make the wrong choice, but whichever you choose, there is doom and danger in both choices. Think of Ridgebrooke as the in between world. Not a place of death, but not a place of life either,' the old man explained. He could tell that they were struggling with the thought of their new reality.

The young couple gazed into each other's eyes and watched the other squeeze their tears out. They clung onto each other's hands like a magnet. Their fate was in their hands. Would they choose to live or die?

NOW

I was trapped and there was nothing I could do. Nobody was telling me anything. They just spoke in riddles. There was no way out of the town. *So, was I just expected to live the rest of my days out here?* I finally sat up after collapsing. *I am a top private investigator, so I need to think like one. Maybe I can go and talk to people? Ask them if they can get out of town or if they are trapped here like me. I cannot give up. Not until all options have been exhausted.* I finally rose to my feet and looked around me suspiciously. I began to head back to the motel, back to where I started. If I wanted to survive this, I needed answers.

Chapter 8

The trek back down to the motel had me feeling overly exhausted. I had realised that no matter what time of day it was in this small town, it always seemed murky, whether it was the sun lighting the sky or the moon. I prepared myself for a judgemental look from Brenda. I knew she would ask why I was still in town and hint that I would not get another room at half price.

I had no idea how long I hadn't slept for, but my whole body felt restless. I entered the motel. I felt as though I had walked back through the gates of hell. With one prompt eye search around the reception, I began to wonder what it was exactly that I was looking for. *What was I expecting to find?*

'You again? I thought you would have come out of the denial stage by now. Looks like I was wrong,' Brenda said, writing in her visitor book behind the desk. *She mentioned denial. Had I found out the town's secret within the tunnel?*

'If you don't mind, I have some questions to ask you,' I insisted.

'Questions? And what would you have to ask me? We have nothing in common! What exactly are you expecting to achieve from this? But fine, enlighten me. Nobody has ever really been interested in my life, so let's see what you come up with,' she answered enthusiastically.

It seemed that now I was taking an interest in her, she wanted to talk. She suddenly seemed more friendly and interested. *But what was I to ask her? I was a private investigator, not a master detective.* I began to act confident in the hope that it would somehow help my enquiries.

'How long have you been here, Brenda?' I asked subtly.

'I have lost count. Nobody counts the days anymore. We don't even sell calendars; I don't know if you have noticed. It is all just one long day until death,' she explained.

The clashing of the visitor's book and the desk startled me and made the hair on the back of my neck stand up forcefully.

'Please, tell me everything you know about Ridgebrooke. I need to know,' I said desperately. I thought she would see it as weakness, but a sudden twinkle of compassion flashed in her eye. I may have been imagining it out of hope.

'Okay, fine, but you must not tell anyone that I told you. They used to call this town "the town of chances" because you only ever came here for a second chance. People from all over America would be just driving or walking along, and they would suddenly be here. It is an old legend, one that I never thought to be true until I was thirty-five. How old do I look now? Sixty? Seventy? God only knows my true age,' she went on, surprisingly opening up to me as I never thought she would.

I grabbed a tattered leather chair from the corner of the motel reception. The leather was flaking off on the sides, and it barely seemed to balance on its wonky four legs. I dragged it up to the desk and unwillingly sat opposite Brenda. She had a story to tell, and I would be the one to benefit from it. I did still fear her wicked looks and eerie presence, but it seemed that the residents of Ridgebrooke were my only chance.

'You do not know your age? Wow that must be ... frightening as well as upsetting,' I sympathised.

'No. We have no emotions here. We are trapped here. It was either go home and die or stay here until I die naturally,' she explained.

I sat curiously staring at her as she spoke. *Did everyone get sent here because they were due to die?* I needed more answers.

'So, you are also trapped here because you were due to die before your time?' I asked.

'Oh yes. At thirty-five, I had just lost my husband. I went on a downward spiral; out of control I was. Drinking every night, doing drugs with youngsters from down the street. I became addicted. I was on my way to meet the dangerous local drug dealer on my bike. A storm came over suddenly with no sign of bad weather beforehand. Then I soon realised, I was in the legend of Ridgebrooke with no way out. I was told if I met with the drug dealer, he would try overcharging me, and when I refused to pay, I would be shot dead. But on a positive note, I have spent years here, probably, and they say I'm due to die around the age of eighty-one by means of pneumonia. I am starting to wonder why I bothered. I keep thinking I should have left when I had the chance and took the drug dealer out somehow. Then I'd have my life back,' she said with more emotion in her eyes than a tortured and damaged soul.

I had a sudden splurge of empathy for her. *She had been trapped here for around twenty years, probably more by her calculations. It didn't seem like she had much of a life either. And she was telling all this to a stranger because she had nobody else. What a lonely life these people had.*

'I am sorry, that is just awful. It sounds like you chose to die a lonely old woman rather than a young addict. Tough decision, definitely. Did you ever … see your double? It sounds strange but I saw myself driving my own car on CCTV. How do you explain that?' I said. I was surprised that she was being so cooperative with me.

'It's all about the rain. I believed it to be just a myth until I saw it for myself. There is some sort of time loop going on here. Whenever the rain comes, some timeframes may cross. It is most likely that you saw yourself driving down the road in your own car because you had gone back to the day you arrived. Instead of reliving it, there are two of you,' she explained.

I had never been more afraid of anything. Spooky just wasn't the word. I had some tough decisions to make, but now it involved time loops.

'Okay … so what are my options here? Be trapped or die?' I asked. I tried to stop the tears from forming in my eyes, but I believed they were still visible.

'I believe you have three options. The first one is you accept your fate. Once you have truly accepted in your heart that you are to die, the rain will somehow take you back to the day you arrived, and you will be out of Ridgebrooke, ready to face your death. Your second option is to build a life here. It's not much of a life. After all these years, I am still afraid, but it's better than being dead. And then there's a third option that nobody has ever dared to attempt before…' she told me as she gazed straight past me.

'Yes? What is it?' I asked, my eyebrows narrowing the more I thought of *nobody has ever dared to attempt it before.*

'Noel, the old man that owns the snack shop. He is the oldest resident here, and he has been here the longest. The golden pocket watch of time has been given to him, making him in charge,' she said.

'Sorry, what? What does that pocket watch have to do with anything?' I asked suspiciously.

'It holds the key to getting out of here. There are many mysteries in this town that none of us have figured out, but as legend has it, that pocket watch is the key to survival. If you press the button on the watch, it stops the rain. So, nothing would be stopping you from escaping. You would be able to go back to your normal life, and you would have a chance to stop your own death. You would take with you all the information that you have now, giving you a better chance of survival. But if anyone is caught near the pocket watch, it wouldn't be good. It is such a precious Ridgebrooke ancient item,' she explained.

Everything relied on a pocket watch. How did it come to this? I now knew that the rain created time jumps that only lasted as long as the rain did. I also knew that the pocket watch may have been my only hope. I either went home and died as I should have or stayed here and lived out my days in an old creepy town, watching this happen to other people. I could have gotten killed trying to get the watch, but I had to take the risk.

I went silent, so she began to speak again.

'How are you supposed to die?' she asked. It almost sounded as though she suddenly cared.

'It's complicated, but my mother was supposed to stab me in the throat as I said goodbye to her on her deathbed. I kept thinking I'd miss her dying, but if the time is messed up here, she is probably still alive. So, I need to ignore all the creepy stuff like the rain messing up time, and possibly being trapped here, and concentrate on getting out. Is that what you are saying?' I said, my eyes widening the more I thought about it.

'Exactly. Nobody has bothered to attempt it because if you are caught, well, you have already signed your death warrant,' she said.

I smiled and stood up. I knew what I needed to do in order to survive, and I would do it. I left the motel and began to march up to the snack shop. I needed that pocket watch to have a chance at surviving, so I would get it at any cost.

Chapter 9

SIX YEARS AGO

I always dreaded the monthly visit. She sat there with her rich tea biscuits and weak cup of tea, glaring at me and judging. Andrew was the only one she was proud of. For twins, we were nothing alike. People used to say I was paranoid, and that a mother's love is for all her children, but they didn't know what I knew. They didn't see the glorified Andrew and all he had achieved.

There was one day when she seemed proud of me, and that was when I became a private investigator. She said, 'Well done' but followed the statement with 'You always love sticking your nose in other people's business, so this job is perfect for you.' I felt stupid thinking she was being genuine at the time.

As I pulled up to her very large and well-kept garden, I noticed my brother's car in the driveway. *He was already here.* I was hoping to speak to my mother alone before he turned up. I had always had a love-hate relationship with my brother. I loved him and everyone else did too, but I hated the feeling of having to compete with him for my mother's affection. But he had a face that you could just not be angry with or jealous of.

So, I never said a word to him about the way I felt, he just assumed I was the perfect sister. I walked up the narrow concrete steps to her home in Sandy Ville, and I knocked on the door loudly to make sure she could hear me.

She was only fifteen years older than us. Being a teenage mum was one thing I admired her for. I could never have imagined what she went through with strict parents. There was a dark thick fog hanging in the air that clung to my chest like a room full of fire and smoke. I entered the house and prepared myself for the lecture I was about to receive.

'Ah, here at last. If you are always late to visit your own mother, I wonder how late you are to work every day,' she said.

Of course, there was no "Hello, Scarlet. How are you doing?" The first thing she said just had to be a complaint.

'Mother. Andrew. I hope you are both … well,' I said miserably. I sat across from them both. If they were any closer on the sofa, it would have looked as though they were cuddling. I sometimes wondered if the umbilical cord ever broke when he was born.

'Of course I'm not well, Scarlet. What a silly thing to say! You know how many health problems I have. And yet you still only visit once a month. Shame on you!' she snarled as she spoke.

Why did she always have to treat me so badly? I did regret the past, so I wish she could have forgiven me for it already. We all had to move on at some point. I often wondered if she really did have a lot of health conditions, or if she said it to make me feel the guilt even more.

'I didn't come here for an argument, Mother. I didn't even want to come. Andrew said I should,' I explained.

The snarl returned. 'Andrew said that because he is a decent man with high morals. He would have never hurt his mother the way you have. You are the devil!' she said as she almost pelted forward on her seat. I felt as though I should have brought some restraints to stop her from launching at me.

'Mother, please. Can we all just have a nice friendly visit with no arguments? I'm tired of being in between you two. I love you both, so please, do it for me,' Andrew said with innocent watery eyes. He still resembled a vulnerable child.

My mother sighed and rolled her eyes. She then stared up to the ceiling instead of making eye contact with me.

'Maybe we should talk through everything that happened. If she still holds a grudge against me, then maybe it's best that everything is out in the open. I can tell she still hates me, so what harm could it do?' I asked, my voice turning slightly aggressive. I knew that I was setting off a firework, and it was out of control. But once I started, I had no off switch.

'Here we go again with the constant self-pity! You need to take some responsibility, Scarlet! You were a troubled teenager, and your actions made me suffer incredibly! Causing me to lose our home, your childhood enemy dying in front of you, and you walked away, making me lose my baby. And that is just the start! You were an evil teenager! You need to realise that these are not the sort of things that I can just forget about or easily forgive. It takes time!' she declared. Her eyebrows kept narrowing. If she continued, they would collapse into her eyes and cause her to be painfully blind.

She brought it up again, I knew she would. Would I ever escape her scorn and judgement? Her eyes were always full of hate.

'But all of that was over ten years ago! I told you what happened with my friend back then, and I regret leaving her to die, I do, but I've changed now. I've got a respectable job, proper friends, and I'm making an effort with the whole family. You cannot punish me forever! I have said sorry over and over for years, and now, I am tired of it!' I screamed as I rose to my feet.

I headed for the front door and felt my brother clasping my arm as I tried to move.

'No, please, Scarlet, don't go. Don't run away every time things get tough! One day, you will be in a situation where you cannot escape. One day, you will have to face your demons!' Andrew called after me.

I turned around to face him with my right hand on the front door handle.

'I'm sorry. I just can't. She thinks I haven't changed since then, and I have. Everyone grows up. I'm not a damaged teenager anymore. If I have to face my demons one day, then so be it, but this is not the way. Goodbye,' I said in a saddened voice.

'Well, if you are going, then don't bother coming back! You are no daughter of mine!' I heard her voice echo as I slammed the door behind me. Hearing her shout viciously like that reminded me of when she used to punish me as a teenager.

If she didn't want me to visit her again, then I wouldn't. I wouldn't go where I wasn't wanted.

NOW

I didn't understand any of it. The rain, the pocket watch, how I even got trapped here in the first place. My only goal was to survive no matter what, but I didn't doubt for a second that the pocket watch would be almost impossible to get my hands on. The daylight was drawing to a close, and the murky night mist was beginning to take over like the moon blocking the sun's natural light. By the time I got to the snack shop, my stomach began to curdle like a bunch of worms were multiplying inside me and getting ready to feed on my intestines.

I hoped he wasn't behind the counter, so I could get the pocket watch and run. But it was never that easy. I could imagine him always having it close by. I walked in, hoping he would have no idea what my plan was.

'Ah, you again. Still here? I'm guessing by now you know why you are here?' Noel said, the old man behind the counter.

'Yes, I am aware, I have been told. I know my past has been worse than good, but I am trying to make it right.' I smiled awkwardly.

'So, let me guess. You thought you would come here and try the alternative plan. I bet Brenda has told you about Lacey and Spencer, hasn't she?' he asked.

My eyebrows formed into a narrowed arch. I felt a burning desire to know more but a feeling of fear overpowered it.

'No? Who are they?' I asked.

'They were the only ones who escaped. They were too young, so I helped them. I broke the rules, but I swore it would never happen again, so forget it. Accept your fate instead,' he answered.

'But Brenda said nobody had ever escaped? She said you never stopped the rain for anyone?' I asked with a curious tone.

'Oh, so she is loyal to some extent then. People around here see her as a busy body. I am retiring if you remember me telling you. I'm retiring because my time is almost up. I am due to die of heart failure in the next few months, so the pocket watch will be passed down to the next oldest resident,' he said.

None of it made any sense still, but I knew enough to understand the type of world that these people were living in. I just hoped that I wouldn't become a part of it.

'Why do you do it? Do you get pleasure by knowing people are due to die and bringing them here to play sick games? Do you love making people suffer in different time periods or something?' I asked.

'It is not me that does that. I don't bring people here. That's the town's business, it will probably always remain a mystery. But the rain is something I have to do to live here and as the oldest resident. If I refused, I would have died straight away. So, yes, me being alive brings terror to others. But show me someone who wouldn't do the same. I help those that deserve it, but it has only ever happened once,' he explained in a monotone voice.

'I don't know how much you know about me, I'm only here because I made a ton of bad mistakes, all of which I regret dearly. Most of them were as a teenager, but I have no excuses for the things I've done. I have had my punishment—through guilt. I don't need to die for it. I need to live, so I can say goodbye to my dying mother. Although she apparently wants to kill me, I still need to be there. My brother wouldn't be able to cope with her death alone. Please. I may be the last person you see going through this before you retire. Wouldn't it be good to help one last broken soul?' I pleaded.

I noticed his eyes weakening with every word. I tried my best to play on his heartstrings because I knew I wouldn't be able to steal the watch. It was as though everyone in this town could see what I was up to. I could see it hanging loose in his pocket. I did mean every word, none of them were lies. I did have good reason to get out of here and change my life. He went silent for a few seconds. I wondered what he was thinking.

'Okay, what is it exactly that you are wanting? I can't promise anything, but I'll try my best. I'll try anything to get out of here safely,' I pleaded.

'Nobody will know I'm dead when I do finally pass away. I chose to stay here and live out my days because I was too much of a coward to face my death at the time. Everyone back home will think I was a missing person that was never found. I know I will have to be buried here, that's how it works but I want a grave in the normal world too. Can you do that? If you survive and live a normal life, can you make sure I have a grave? I just want to know that in the end, I'll be back where I belong,' he explained with his narrow eyes filling up.

I felt the pain pouring from his words. It seemed like a small price to pay to get control of that watch. It would cost me a pretty penny to get a gravestone, but it would be nothing compared to being stuck here like him. I had plenty of money in my savings account, I would pay any price to be given a second chance. It would be an easy resolve.

'Done. If that's what you want in exchange for helping me out of here, then that is fine. I just need to go home. I'm desperate,' I replied.

'Right, okay looks like you have a deal. I just want my family to be able to grieve for me. Make up a story that you are an old friend of mine, you'll think of something. Just give me the funeral I deserve, yeah? Okay, the next rain pour is due in a few minutes. I can only hold it off for so long before people get suspicious. I need you to go to your car and drive to the entrance of Ridgebrooke, right near the sign. As soon as you see the rain drops falling just stop, close your eyes. When you wake up, you should be out of here,' he explained.

Was he really that desperate to get a grave out of here that he'd do this for a stranger? Could I trust him? Was it some sort of trick? After all that struggling to try and get out, would this really work? I guess I had no choice but to try.

I thanked him and walked out. I began to run down the street towards my car. It was where I had left it because it was dry weather. I got in and began to drive towards the exit of Ridgebrooke. As soon as I got to the sign, I slammed my brakes on and parked there. I hoped with everything I had that this worked. I closed my eyes and waited for a miracle.

Chapter 10

15 YEARS AGO

I sat and watched them all pass by. Some of them tossed us the odd 20p coin, others just laughed. Why did we have to do this here where people knew us? I had just turned 16 and she kept hinting for me to leave home, but we had all left home. And not by our own choice.

'You really are a waste of space. We wouldn't be sitting here begging on the streets if you didn't steal from me! You wretch!' Her voice was deep and sinister. *She would never let me get over this.*

'I didn't think we would lose our home, okay? It was just a bit of fun. You never gave me money when I needed it, so I took it. Figured you had plenty left,' I sniggered.

Our clothes were beginning to smell, that awful damp, unclean smell. One of my mother's old friends said she knew of a place that we could stay. It was the rough side of town, but the houses looked pretty big on the outside. But they couldn't sort it for a few more days and there was nowhere else for us to go.

Yesterday, we had to share a sandwich between the three of us that a polite lady graciously gave us. How embarrassing. I had learnt my lesson not to steal money, but she kept punishing me anyway. She just had to keep going over the finer details to watch the guilt drain my face over and over.

'Please, this is bad enough. We shouldn't go through all this again. I am just so sorry you lost your house mother; you loved that house,' Andrew interjected.

She turned to Andrew and gave him a quick peck on the top of his head, something she had never once done to me. *Did I really care?*

'Thank you my precious. At least one of my children are grateful. When you get a high paid career, you will look after your mother, I know you will. My sweet boy,' she answered.

I watched them keeping each other warm, leaving me on the cold, dirty ground alone and scared. I knew I caused this, but did I really deserve this punishment? She would pay for all she had put me through one day. She wouldn't be the demon I feared forever.

NOW

I felt a sharp sting the corner of my eye as I woke. I found my head pressed against the steering wheel of my car. *Where was I?* My head shot up when I remembered. *I was trying to escape Ridgebrooke.* I immediately observed my surroundings. There was no winding road, no Ridgebrooke sign, or creepy buildings. I was out! I had to be. I looked up at the house my car was parked in front of. *I was at my mum's house.* I looked down at the clock in my car.

I wanted to know if I would get questioned on where I had been all this time. It said 13th April 2022. Yes! I had done it. It was almost as if everything in Ridgebrooke never happened. I quickly got out of my car before my brother and mum started to suspect something. I locked it swiftly and ran to the front door. I knocked loudly, hoping I hadn't missed my chance to say one last goodbye.

Then, I remembered. *She wanted to kill me. I got sent to Ridgebrooke for one last chance. I had to be on guard at all times and watch out for any sharp objects near her.* Andrew came to the door to greet me, his head hung loose like a sad bear cub that had been separated from its mother.

'There you are! You'd better come in; it's getting really late now. She doesn't have long left. She has been wanting to see you,' he said respectfully. *I bet she only wanted to see me to end me. Her lifelong hatred for me had finally come to the surface.*

I walked past him, and I heard the door drift shut behind me. I felt a cold shiver run through me when I looked around the house that I grew up in as a teen. The one I hadn't stepped inside for six years. The wallpaper hadn't been changed since I was a teenager when we first moved here. A golden floral wallpaper with bright green leaves. The edges were peeling off, and the stains of my past haunted the walls.

I had never felt comfortable in the home ever since those days. Andrew put his hand out to point me to the stairs. I suddenly thought, *should I really go up there and be alone with her? What if she has hidden a weapon somewhere? Why is her dying wish to kill her only daughter instead of forgiving me?*

I didn't want to alarm Andrew or cause a scene, so I walked up the old creaky stairs and pretended that everything was fine. I somehow remembered to avoid the large crack in the fourth step, as I had memories of almost breaking my ankle on it at least once a week. Andrew somehow always managed to avoid that side of the step. Possibly because my mother cared enough to remind him about it constantly. I tried to shake off the bad memories and give my full attention to the dangerous present.

The smell was exactly the same. Cheap air freshener and the faint smell of freshly baked bread. Even though I doubted that she had baked anything in a while. I saw the almost black painted wall with a crack in the paint work that always reminded me of a lightning bolt, and I knew it was her bedroom.

I knew her eyes would be all over me, observing and judging from the minute I walked into the room. Even when she was close to death, she would be devious. I placed my hand on the handle and forced myself in. The door opened slowly to reveal my disease-ridden mother bit by bit, and it forced me to hold my breath. So much so that I felt my body draining of oxygen as though my lungs were shrinking.

'She finally decides to show herself. Why so late? Did you want to make sure you watched me draw my last breath?' she said, her voice making a crackling noise in my ears.

'No, mother. I am here to make my peace and say goodbye. I want you to go knowing we are okay,' I answered. I sat myself down at the bottom of her bed, fearing to be so close.

'Okay? Is that what this is? More like so you can have a clear conscience! This has nothing to do with me. You feel too guilty about the past, so you've come here to make yourself feel better and watch me die!' She yelled. *I had never seen her look so weak. She was always strong-willed and aggressive.*

'Whatever you think of me, I have gone through a lot to get here. I know I could have done better by visiting, but after that argument six years ago, I thought you hated me for the past, so I didn't bother, but I'm here now, and I want us to make up properly,' I said, anticipating the moment that she would try to kill me.

No. It was impossible. I looked at her, and she was clearly defenceless! She was lying in bed in a vomit-covered nightgown, and she could barely sit up. There was no way she could have killed me. Maybe they got it wrong?

'You want me to forgive you, so Andrew will be kind to you once I'm gone. How can I forgive you? For making me lose my baby, for making me lose my parents' family home, for being so cruel to me for years. How? Tell me because I don't know!' She sniggered.

'Mum, I was a teenager, still a child! I didn't know that things would end that badly. I was just being defiant, but I learnt my lesson!' I yelled as I felt my anger slowly building up. I promised myself that I would be kind to her in her final hours.

'You didn't know things would end badly? Constantly stealing money that I needed for the mortgage, which eventually made us homeless. Then throwing things around and causing me to lose your baby sister. How are they forgivable? You KILLED your own sister before she even had the chance to live! You caused us to live in this cheap rotting house! You being born ruined my life, and it's about time you paid for it!' she screamed. I heard her bones crack as she clenched her body and almost sat up as she spoke.

About time I paid for it? This was it; she was going to try and kill me! The people of Ridgebrooke were right. If I wanted to live, I had to try and stop her! She viciously clasped me into her frail, skinny arms and ragged me towards her. *This was it.*

I tried to wriggle away from her, but she was surprisingly strong when she looked so weak. *She was determined to end me.* I looked down to where the knife could be, then I noticed the quilt cover twitching and moving slightly. The room fell silent with tension. She suddenly pulled out the carving knife that she used to use when I was younger for the weekly family dinner.

'Mum! What are you doing, put that down!' I gasped. I grabbed her arm and shoved it to one side, out of my face.

I hoped that I could shut this down with reasoning. Play on her maternal instincts if *she had any*. Well, she did for Andrew. Andrew! He was the way out of this, he was just downstairs! He would never believe me if I said our mother had drawn a knife on me while on her deathbed. He thought too highly of her. But I had to think of something!

'Please, Mum! Put the knife down. You cannot kill me; I am your daughter! We can work this out!' I yelled down her ear.

Her force against me became greater. It seemed that the only thing she was passionate about doing before she passed was to kill me. It was almost as if nothing else in the world mattered except this moment. *I couldn't let a dying woman overpower me, I had to do something.* I stretched forward with all my strength and reached for the lamp at her bedside.

With one swift hand movement, I took it into my grasp. *I had to take full control or die; there was no other option. It was her or me.* With all of my strength, I smashed the lamp against her temple. The impact made me scrunch my body into a heap of disgust. *Was this really who I was? A killer?* Her head hit the pillow and sunk into it, the blood completely taking over the faded pattern, soaking it through. I gasped, I panicked, I squirmed. I gently leaned over her body, checking for any signs of life. *She was gone.* Her eyes firmly open, facing the wall. She had died instantly by my hand.

I looked down and tried to focus on the murder weapon that I was still clinging onto, the lamp. I felt my hands weaken, losing their grip. My whole body turned weak, frail. I was unable to move or process what I had done. Yes, it was self-defence but that didn't make it feel any better.

I tried to focus but everything went fuzzy and unrecognisable. I was thrown back into reality when the sound of the lamp crashing against the floorboards stunned me. *Andrew would have heard that, he would come to check on her.* What would he do when he realised that I had killed our mother?

Chapter 11

'Mum? Scarlet? Are you two all right up there?' Andrew yelled from the bottom of the stairs. His voice echoed like a lion's roar in the lonely wild. I stared at her lifeless body and the blood stains. *What could I do? Even if I lied to him, he'd know.* I felt my mouth immediately open to respond, but I was instantly distracted by not knowing what to say. *Surely, if it's silent and neither of us answer, he will think it's suspicious. Would he understand if I told him?*

I then heard steady rhythmic footsteps coming up the stairs. He was silent so surely; he knew that something was wrong. *Surely,* he didn't trust us in the same room together for this long. The sound of his footsteps sent me into a panicking frenzy, I quickly grabbed her body and dragged it to face me. I immediately felt startled to have her eyes staring into my soul, judging me. *But I had to hide the blood on her temple, this was the only way.* He was probably expecting a quick goodbye from me, and then I'd walk back out. Just moments later, the door opened slightly. I couldn't breathe with shock and the distasteful flavour of vomit clung to the back of my throat, but I somehow forced myself to act normal.

'Mother! No! I promised I'd be here for her last breath!' Andrew yelled. The tears immediately poured from his red, tired eyes.

'I am sorry, Andrew. She went peacefully,' I told him. The lie caused me to silently choke on my words. *Could he see my pain?* His eyes suddenly fell to the floor below me.

'The lamp! She loved that lamp! It was our grandmothers. How did it fall off?' Andrew asked, his attention turning from his dead mother to the lamp.

'I don't know. I must have knocked it off accidently when I realised she had passed away, sorry.

Maybe I should leave, give you some time with her alone,' I said. I forced myself to find the strength to stand, but my legs went from beneath me, and I almost fell to the ground.

'Scarlet! You are not as strong as you make out, her death is getting to you, I can tell. Come on, let's get you a drink. We have some of that sparkling water you love,' he said calmly. He gently took my hand and guided me out of the bedroom and down each step of the stairs. A horrid guilt washed over me as I realised, *he thought the way I was acting was due to me grieving for our mother.* I guess he never truly understood how evil I could be.

I sat at the kitchen table, and he rushed over to the counter and prepared a drink for me, his hands visibly shaking even from a short distance. He took out another glass and poured some tap water for himself. It took longer than I expected but maybe he was shaken up after seeing his beloved mother dead like that. I was too busy trying to process what I had just done. The bond between my brother and I was firmly broken forever, like an umbilical cord being torn out of us. I could never speak the truth to him again, not after this. I didn't have the heart to tell him that if I drank fizzy water, I would bring it straight back up. I needed plain water. But he must have felt as though he needed to be helpful and keep himself busy, so I let him get me a drink. What harm could it have done?

'Here, drink this. You look like you need it. I'll call the coroner soon,' he insisted.

I took the glass from him but when he began to pace the room and his back was to me, I swapped our glasses. Maybe he wouldn't realise until I was gone that he would be drinking my favourite sparkling water that he hated. I just needed plain, refreshing water but the minute I mentioned that I couldn't stomach my favourite drink, he would be suspicious. I happily downed the contents before he could realise. The water was extra refreshing, quenching my thirst and helping me to get my strength back after such a violent encounter. *Wait. A coroner? Why?*

'Sorry, did you say a coroner? Why do you need to call them? We know what she died of,' I asked. I placed the empty glass on the table and waited for his response.

'You know why,' Andrew said, his voice turning raspy and frightening. I looked up at him, giving him a look of fear. *How did he know? Did he really know?*

'I'm sorry, I don't know what you mean. You're in shock, you're not making sense,' I told him.

'Please don't act like you're innocent in all of this. I know what you've done,' he answered. His voice remained unfriendly, cold. What was he up to? *Did he know? How?*

'What? I...' I couldn't find the words to finish my sentence. Somehow, he would see right through me. I hadn't prepared myself for if he found out. I at least thought it would take a few days.

'Because of you, I won't have any family left. But I am doing this for her. She knew what you'd do when you saw her in such a vulnerable state, I should have listened, but I told her you had good in you, I was wrong. Now it's your turn to feel what she felt in her final moments. How's the sparkling water? Feeling...dizzy yet?' He asked.

What was he hinting at? Did he promise our mother that he would...kill me? Did me escaping Ridgebrooke do nothing to change my fate? As the words swirled around in my mind, I couldn't decide what to ask first. I hadn't got this far to be taken down by anyone, even if it was my own brother.

'No. Why would I be feeling dizzy? What are you talking about?' I asked, hoping this was a moment of madness for him and nothing else.

'She was the only person who truly looked out for me. She had hours left in her yet plus the blood stains on the lamp gave it away. It's over for you, I'm sorry but this is how it has to end. I gave you a friendly poison, nothing aggressive it just sends you into a deep sleep that you never wake up from. Goodbye, sister,' he explained.

My own brother had tried to poison me. *Tried.* He hadn't realised yet that I changed our glasses. I had never been more grateful for my sudden desire for plain tap water.

'You don't understand what I've been through, and I survived it! She had to go; she would have killed me otherwise! But you! You trying to poison me for her is unforgiveable. I didn't drink the fizzy water; I switched our glasses. Looks like the little plan of yours is falling apart. What are you going to do now without mummy's evil input?' I mocked, an evil fire began to rise within me, something I didn't know existed until this moment.

A look of frustration came over him, one I had never witnessed in his eyes before. I was in danger. I had overcome the obstacle of my mother but now my brother was willing to end my life in her memory. I leaned down and grabbed my empty glass from the table and I bounced it off the wall behind him. Anything to create a distraction. I watched the explosion of glass behind him as he ducked down, trying to dodge the damage. As he folded into himself to avoid the flying glass, I headed straight for the front door, swiping his keys from the passageway hook as I went by. I heard his pounding footsteps far behind me, but I didn't give him the chance to catch up. I knew I had it in me to escape, this was nowhere near as mind bending as Ridgebrooke. I had the advantage; I was stronger, wiser and faster than he ever was.

My trembling hands managed to lock the door behind me, and I ran to my car, throwing myself into it and immediately starting the engine. I noticed his shadow at the front door, knocking and screaming. I chose to ignore him. I wouldn't kill two family members in one day, I'd do what I did best. *Run. Survive. Start a new life.* Leaving Ridgebrooke was my chance to become a better person and I had failed. I would forever live-in fear of being taken back there with no escape next time. I drove down the road, wondering how long Andrew would be locked in our mother's home before he broke a window to get out, but I'd be long gone by then. I had killed my own mother; Andrew had almost killed his own sister. Maybe we weren't as different as we both thought after all. Maybe we would meet again in Ridgebrooke, *one day.*

STORY 2

THE AFTER WORLD

Chapter 1

8th May: 3002

They were wrong. Some of us were still breathing. They promised to find a way to fix it, but they couldn't. I thought I would start a diary to document everything that I have witnessed so far, to mark history for the future generation. Right now, on Earth, 354 people occupy the planet. Compared to the 12 billion that we shared it with before.

We were all warned. Spirits in the night, shadows in the dark, but we refused to listen. Now, I, Kalina Rayland, must continue to do whatever is asked of me in order to stay alive. We are alive, but can anyone really call this a life? Sometimes, just breathing isn't enough. Yalford Valley is our home, and we have been blessed by its survival. Nobody knows how the town still exists, but they will find out eventually.

The year is 3002, and just 3 years ago, in 2999, our precious home, Earth, had met its end. Or so everyone thought. The heavy pollution caused global warming to become unbearable, and once that happened, there was no turning back. The ozone layer, which once protected us from the sun's UV radiation, was so significantly damaged that billions of us were killed. It started with soaring temperatures.

We had to have cooling rooms in our homes at first and not leave that room for more than 10 minutes, or we would burn. It sometimes lasted weeks. Water became a rare sight. Thousands died from heat complications within the first month. But within weeks, the world heated up so much that there was a gigantic explosion, killing everyone on the planet. Except the 354 people in space at the time of the explosion. A space tour hadn't been known for long, only about 27 years, but my family and I were excited to go and see it, despite it costing an absolute fortune.

My sister and I went while my husband stayed on Earth and took care of our twin sons. When we landed back on earth, we had nothing to go home to. The plants were dead, all the animals were dead, and a whole population of people were dead. My sons and my husband were gone.

The pain of my loss was so intense that I had to use my maiden name. I couldn't hear his name. It made my eardrums want to explode and bleed. I had just turned 31 when the explosion happened, and that was 3 years ago. I doubt anybody but me even bothers to keep track of the days.

But I thought it was time to start recording everything that we have gone through. I hope someone will read this in hundreds of years. It means the human race managed to survive and our sacrifices were not for nothing. You should know what this life is like. It's not like I'm completely alone. My older sister is still here with me, but we just don't connect anymore. She's changed. The disaster changed everyone.

I know what you are thinking as you read this. We are lucky. Some might say we are, but I just feel broken and empty. It is so lonely down here. There is nothing to do all day except sit and think about how life used to be. It's amazing that we've even survived this long.

The first year after the explosion was the worst. We kept trying to grow crops, but they just kept dying. We had tornados that were made with fire instead of wind. The wind was no longer a gentle breeze but like a blaze of flames from a campfire. We constantly ran low on oxygen, and we risked our skin being burnt every time we were outside.

There were a lot more plants now, but they had to go through evolution to survive such strong weather conditions. The only time we could collect water was when it rained because the rivers nearby were more like volcanos. Everything was a risk. Everything was full of heat and fire. It was a surprise that we had survived this long.

The new people in charge who called themselves the 'The Rulers' brought everything from their space tour down to Earth, so we could have more oxygen when the plant count was too low. If it wasn't for their quick thinking, we'd all be dead. Although some people are far from grateful for their hard work at keeping us alive.

There was also enough food to last us a year and a half until the trees began to grow once again. Some now believe that Earth is truly recovering. But it will only take one more wave like the last one to kill us all and make our progress worth nothing. It was up to us to make mankind survive this. There were constant news reports, the government begged us all to reduce our carbon footprint to save the planet while we still had the chance, but many refused. This was what it cost us.

Humans ruined this Earth, and we almost faced extinction. People didn't know what to think in times of disaster. There are so many conspiracies as to why we were the ones to survive. I do not believe such stories, but some believe that we were hand-picked by a greater power, as we were the better humans of them all. But agreeing with that would mean I was saying that I deserved to live while my family did not, and that was something I couldn't accept.

In recent weeks, there has been an uprising. People believed that it was time to put a new government in place and rebuild what we once had. The Rulers had been in charge for 3 years. They assumed power as soon as we got back to Earth. Ever since, nobody has tried to overthrow them, as they did help us to survive. But now things were getting out of hand. The rules that were put into place to apparently save us were making our lives more of a misery each day.

Some rules such as 'you are only allowed to eat healthy foods so that you may live longer' was understandable and most of the time it did work. But now the leaders wanted to rule our whole lives for us. They wanted to pick our romantic partner for us, and we must reproduce excessively, or we will be put to death.

There was a sudden desperate need to bring more humans onto the planet, and therefore, every woman over 16 must be married and have at least 5 children. Yes, the death penalty has returned and is used way more than it used to be. If you refused to do as the Rulers said, it would be an instant death sentence.

If you were sensible enough, you just went along with the rules and tried your best not to draw attention to yourself. But surely killing people when we were so short of life was a bad choice, but they saw it as a must to keep absolute control. We weren't even allowed outside alone because outside of Yalford Valley was too dangerous, even though nobody really explained why that was.

My sister, Josephine Rayland, was a member of the Rulers. There were 5 of them, 3 men and 2 women. I kept trying to talk her out of these new rules, but the more I spoke about it, the more she dismissed me as a person, not just my opinions. So, I had to leave her to it. I had no idea why she chose to join them, but, in her eyes, it was that or death. I am starting to think that maybe she had a point. The Rulers had more freedom than any of us.

Nobody cared about what your life was like before this happened. Now that these new rules were in place, nobody was allowed to be single. I am due to meet my new partner next week. Apparently, he is a 55-year-old man named Cyrus Cusack. He had a wife before all of this happened, but she died 4 years before of liver failure. Therefore, he was a widow. But in the new law's eyes, he was single.

It was just another day in Yalford Valley. People were singing as a substitute for music, men were building new sheds and tending the crops. Women were finding new health remedies from new herbs and plants and cooking as best as they could. The children were running around and playing. The 5-person government stayed in a small shack to plan how else they would control us. I wanted my sister to be an informer for me, but she was too loyal; she would have never betrayed her job.

If anyone could see this town, it would just look like the world was populated as before. The streets were always full, the small houses and shacks were occupied, and businesses ran as they used to. But the difference was, it was all made by us. The mystery of Yalford Valley continued to interrupt sleep and cause living nightmares. I guess we would never really know what forces were really upon us. There were so many secrets hidden in this new land, only time would tell.

Chapter 2

11th May: 3002

The night breeze continued to mark our land. The darkness that hung over us swept our town, undiscovered.

'There you are, Kalina! Come, I have to show you your new fiancé!' my sister, Josephine, shouted at me as she hooked my arm and rushed me over to a tall grey-haired man who waited patiently for me.

'Oh, you must be Kalina Rayland, what a beauty! I am Cyrus Cusack. We are to be married in just a few days,' Cyrus said while smiling brightly at me. I didn't want to marry him, but I don't think anybody wanted the Rulers to pick their lovers either.

'You may not want this marriage, but I will do anything to make it work,' Cyrus continued as I just stared at him and didn't reply. I then looked at my sister and dragged her to one side to get her alone.

'You and the other rulers cannot force me to be with someone who I'm not even attracted to. I at least want someone my own age!' I pleaded, trying to keep my voice down as I felt disgusted, but I wanted to seem polite.

Josephine shrugged her shoulders and crossed her arms aggressively.

'That is out of my hands, you will do as we say or … well, you know the consequences. Everyone has a part to play in repopulating the Earth. I am already pregnant with Grindon Hilton's child. I told him, as he is the boss, that I wanted to do my part, and he offered to get me pregnant, and I agreed,' Josephine replied, looking quite proud of herself. I shook my head and couldn't believe what I was hearing.

'So, you get to pick the father of your baby but nobody else does? What is fair about that? Maybe you should reconsider being my informer, you never know, it may help having someone on the inside,' I asked. I could see Cyrus glaring over. She laughed to herself.

'No, absolutely not. I'm not risking my position for anything or anyone, not even my own sister. Now come on. It's nightfall. It's time for the execution of the week,' Josephine said as she escorted me and my future husband over to 'The Stage'. The Stage where 'criminals' were tortured to death until they died in front of every single one of us.

We were only allowed out after dark. To be out during the day was too risky. There was a 75% chance that you could burn to death just by being outside for 20 minutes. Whoever had to go outside during the day had to be covered from head to toe in thick fireproof armour. There was a giant cover, which hung over our town like a dark cloud. It took 4 months to put up, and it was above the whole town so that we were constantly protected from the sun.

Of course, the sun could get through it, but not enough to kill us. Not straight away anyway. Nobody really knew the long-term health effects of our situation. Although some people claimed to know. Now that there was no ozone layer, there was an even bigger risk of developing skin cancer. A cure for cancer was found in 2086, but since technology has been wiped out, we wouldn't be able to save anyone who got it. We did have more people, but 16 were lost from instant skin burns, flame tornadoes, and skin cancer. We weren't willing to make the same mistakes.

Sometimes, we were allowed out during the day, depending on the sun's angle and the radiation percentage, but it was quite rare. In fact, it was so rare that hardly any of us even remember what it was like. It only ever happened once when people claimed that the Earth was recovering. But they were wrong. It was too risky, so nobody has dared to go out in the daylight ever since. We weren't allowed to go many places, even outside of the town though, just a few small shops and The Stage where the executions took place. Executions took place at night, and by law, everyone in the town had to attend. My sister pushed to the front for a good view of the execution. I always felt sick to my stomach to watch such horrible torture; even the children had to witness it.

'This 17-year-old woman, Prescott Willows, has come here on this night to die. She has been married for a year and a half, and she has been pregnant on two occasions, both of which, she miscarried. We cannot stand by as a community and watch such failures, as we need new babies to repopulate. One failed attempt at producing can be tolerated, but one after another is breaking the law.'

He continued, 'There are serious accusations from her husband, Lars Willows, as he suggests that Mrs Willows failed to reproduce on purpose, as she believes she is too young to be a mother. We no longer ask whether she is guilty or not, but she now must suffer a painful death for killing two of her own babies. She will suffer capital punishment, death,' Grindon Hilton announced as he stood on The Stage next to the criminal. I thought about my sister's new pregnancy for a second. Surely being 37 and pregnant came with its own risks. If she miscarried, that could be her up there in a few months.

In the old world, miscarrying was a tragedy, not a crime. Why would this young woman want her own babies dead when she knew it was the only thing that could save her? Grindon finished the ceremony speech, and then he got out his execution box. The box held 2 giant carving knives, a sledgehammer, some acid, and a stick, which they set on fire. It was up to Grindon as the leader of the Rulers to pick how each person should die based on how bad their crime was.

He believed that not telling us how she would die created extra suspense and made it more interesting, but this wasn't entertainment to me. Not many other people seemed to want to witness this either. Prescott Willows was tied to a thick wooden pole, so she couldn't move. Her mouth was gagged, so we couldn't feel her pain when she cried out. How could they do this to someone? Especially someone who was innocent.

Grindon took out the largest knife, and he stood in front of Prescott, and we heard half screams as she attempted to scream through the gag, but it was never loud enough. As soon as Grindon moved away from her, we could see what was being done. Many heads turned the other way, but I just couldn't look away.

I was too disgusted to speak but too upset to not look her in the eyes as she said goodbye to the world. A large slit was made in her upper abdomen where her bowels had been viciously torn from her body. Blood poured down her white dress and splattered onto the floor of The Stage.

Her bowels were thrown on the ground next to her for all to see. They fell neatly and spread across The Stage. I could see Prescott staring at her own bowels. I could tell that her consciousness was slipping away. He then used that same knife to viciously gash at her throat until we could almost see the muscles in her neck. We were forced to watch her choke on her own blood as it began to trickle onto The Stage. Surely our destiny wasn't to survive just so we could kill each other.

She was then untied. She fell to her knees, and we had no choice but to watch her bleed out. But we all knew that Prescott taking her last breath was not the end of the horror show. I saw the sledgehammer towering over her skull, and then it ploughed into the base of her skull with a distinct sound of cracking and crunching. Grindon continued the act over and over until her head looked nothing more than a squashed, bruised watermelon. The blood splattered all over the front row of people watching and on my sister's face.

She wiped it from her cheek gracefully as though brutal murder was her favourite pastime. Grindon didn't stop there. He didn't stop until every single bone in her body was broken, and she no longer looked human but rather a pile of guts, bones, and blood. I never saw the point in dragging out the torture. She was already dead and mutilating her body was unnecessarily evil. But it was all for show. The Rulers wanted to make sure that we knew what punishment looked like. Despite everything, my sister was still willing to bring Grindon's child into the world after watching him torture and kill people. I then tried to walk away, but Josephine grabbed my arm and dragged me towards her.

'Just for trying to walk away from what everyone must see; you will scrub this girl's blood with your own hands. Go and get a cloth to clean this, ready for next week,' Josephine said to me dominantly, as I was too afraid to refuse. Refusing a member of the Rulers was instant death. I looked at her, but I didn't dare to answer back. I had already tried that today and risked my life to do so. I walked away from the horrified crowd to go to the small cabin where we held our supplies of cotton and linen.

I grabbed the nearest brown cloth on the pile, and I thought about what I had just seen. I had seen so many executions, but they were all just as shocking as the last. I constantly watched over my shoulder as I strolled in the dark alone. I could always feel a presence lurking over me. It was something that I couldn't explain. Something made me walk quicker whenever I walked past a dark alleyway. It wasn't just because they were out of bounds. It was because each time I walked past; I felt a rush run through me.

A cold shiver ran from the back of my neck to the bottom of my spine. It was near impossible that I could have been cold, as it was always at least 30 degrees in Yalford Valley.

'Be with us,' I heard a voice whisper in the shadows of the mysterious alleyway. For a second, I believed I was hearing things. I tried to look closer into the dark depths of the alleyway, but it was too dark to see anything.

I was desperate to see who was trying to reach me from the shadows, but I was startled by my sister.

'Hurry up with that cloth, sis, the blood will stain!' I heard my sister shout as I shot out of the alleyway and ran back to The Stage. I quickly walked up to The Stage as my hands shook in fear. I had always feared this job and felt glad whenever someone else had to do it instead.

Two other women came up to me and helped me scrub the blood away from The Stage. We never spoke when we did this. It was a task that everyone just wanted to be over. We scrubbed until we could only see the stains that never came out. Once most of the blood was gone, I threw the cloth down onto The Stage for someone else to take care of. As I attempted to turn around, I almost bumped heads with a man.

I looked past him and noticed that the crowd had cleared. I was going to walk past him until I recognised him from the space tour. He had attempted to flirt when he first met me, but we hadn't spoken since. He was a 39-year-old man named Kaiser Everts. I heard they were pairing him up with a new partner too.

'Oh, it's Kaiser, right?' I asked awkwardly as we just stared at each other. He laughed and nodded.

'Hi, you remember me! I'm sorry, I don't mean to be rude, but my future wife is expecting me back at the house,' he replied, even though there were no houses anymore. We just had sheds, huts, and small cabins. We usually said houses because it made it feel more like before. I tried to look sympathetic about Kaiser being forced to marry someone, but I remembered that it was the new norm.

'Oh, so I'm not the only one being married off then. See you around,' I said casually as a member of the Rulers came up to us. Possibly because we were the only ones left near The Stage.

'Do not speak to each other. You both need to go to your homes. It's nearly the turning in time, 11 p.m.,' Edgar Kelton announced while looking smug. I sighed, and Kaiser walked off awkwardly.

'Oh, so you people even control who we speak to now? Where is the freedom?' I asked, probably overstepping the mark. If I continued to question them, they would put me to death as well. He didn't even answer me, he just walked me to my small cabin. My small cabin was nothing more than a badly constructed wooden bed and a box-sized room for a toilet. It resembled a prison cell.

We didn't even have our own kitchens to cook in anymore. We all had to be in our 'homes' by 11 p.m., otherwise, we would have to answer to Grindon the next day. I had been living this horrible excuse of a life for too long. Things needed to change. But what could I do?

Chapter 3

3 YEARS AGO

'I'm sure you all feel privileged to be up here and get a very expensive tour of space. The people of Yalford Valley, I welcome you to Mars,' Grindon said to everyone as I stared at Mars with amazement.

We were chauffeured around space in an upmarket giant globe that resembled a bauble. It was hung on by an overhead metal line, so we floated calmly in the atmosphere. It was full of fresh oxygen, expensive party food, and cocktails. It seemed that every citizen of Yalford Valley had come. It could hold a maximum of 500 people, but the tour went around every town in England, and people got to sign their name down and pay 6 thousand pounds.

A few people from our town were left behind, as they just couldn't afford the trip. My husband wanted to come with us, but he had urgent business to attend to that was unavoidable. Our two three-year-old boys were too young to leave the Earth. My sister and I peacefully watched Mars in awe as we listened to Grindon's speech about all the research that was relevant to Mars from the last 500 years.

It was beautiful with so much to look at. It was astonishingly overwhelming. We had the Earth to look at on one side and Mars on the other. But the amazing view was disturbingly interrupted. My ears almost burst with the sound of an unthinkable explosion.

I tried to turn my head and see what had caused it, but it was too bright to look at. I had to squint and look away. We could almost feel the heat forcing its way through the glass that proved to be our only protector. Some people screamed with fear and some people cried in shock.

I remembered wishing it wasn't true. Our beloved Earth was burning right in front of our eyes.

No water, no land. Just pure orange fire and puffs of black smoke. It looked more like the sun. The floating globe began to shake from the impact and most of us fell to the ground, but the thick glass didn't break. Luckily, we were a safe distance away when it happened. It was safe to say that nobody on Earth could have survived that.

All I could think about was my husband and sons, burning to death and suffering. I cried, of course, I cried. Most of the people around me did as well. There was a massive panic. Everyone was rushing around asking, 'What shall we do now?' and 'Can we survive up here?' and 'We can't go back down there.' They were then all stopped when the leader of the tour, Grindon, blew his loud whistle.

'Yalford Valley people! Please listen! It appears that the news was correct. The Earth's ozone layer is now gone. We were warned, but not many of us chose to listen. All we can do now is pray for our own survival. I know this is a shock to us all, but we are currently the only surviving members of the human race. We cannot give up. We are the last ones standing. As soon as it is safe and the fire and smoke clears, we need to get back down there and find a new way to live. But we need to take precautions and be prepared. The temperatures will be unbearable. The crops will keep dying. We have enough food and clean unpolluted oxygen in here to last us about a year on Earth. It's a good job we brought this much food because it is officially our only way to survive. We will go back when it's safe to land on Earth without us burning to death too,' Grindon told us. I tried to listen, but none of it felt real. They were right. The end had come.

NOW

16th May: 3002

Ideally, I didn't really want to write a diary, but things could get worse in the future, and this may end up being the only record of everything that happens.

I had been thinking all day about what life was like before everyone died but I act strong in real life and pretend nothing bothers me. I kept thinking about how I was only around because I was an experiment. I was genetically made in a science lab. They got to choose my intelligence level, my looks, my memory capacity and even some traits.

The procedure was successful, and it became popular. That's just how advanced technology had become before all of this, but it was all gone now. When I went to school, I did history, and I learnt all about a thousand years ago, and the way in which technology had developed since then was astonishing. Some people even took a capsule that stopped them from ageing because it was possible.

The death rate had fallen by 64% because scientists and doctors were constantly finding new medications and new ways to stop the biological ending of the human body. There were people that were living to 150 years old, which of course, made the population even bigger. The man who made me also found a way to make a woman give birth with no pain and no complications, and he could even speed up a baby's development so that a woman could give birth quicker. We had gotten used to an easy lifestyle. Nobody had to do manual jobs because technology took care of it all. It was mainly business careers and the creative industries that thrived.

Scientists had known for centuries just how bad climate change was getting. They realised that we couldn't rescue the Earth if not everyone was willing to change. But in 2980, they found us somewhere else to live. Another planet for the human race to ruin. It was somewhere that humans could live on, and they had found a way to get us there.

Unfortunately, all of the rockets and ships that would get us to the other planet were also blown up in the giant explosion. The predictions regarding when the explosion would happen were 2 years out, and we just weren't prepared. I didn't know why I spent so much time thinking of what my life used to be like.

I got married just 2 days ago. I married Cyrus because if I didn't, my sister threatened that I would be next to be executed, and I didn't want to risk that. I didn't really know what lengths she would go to just to show how loyal she was to her colleagues. It was a very quick and boring marriage.

Romance was absent, of course, and there was nobody there but my sister and a priest. I didn't get to wear a wedding dress, but not many people did when things were normal anyway. Traditional wedding ceremonies were classed as 'too old fashioned' when I was about 5 years old in 2968, and people just got married the way they wanted to.

Nothing was like the old world, and some people did prefer it that way, but I would give anything to spend my days with my husband and my children. Technically, we were all dying. Radiation from the sun's ultraviolet rays were killing us, but because of our attempt to protect ourselves from it, it was killing us slowly. The two doctors that we have here said it would take anywhere from 6 months to 10 years. We had been here for 3 years, and so far, only 3 people had died from it. Everyday they're trying to find new possible ways of stopping it from killing us.

They are waiting for one of the married ladies to have a baby, so they can run tests on the baby's DNA and see how the radiation affects their skin, as they could have evolved a higher tolerance to it. There had been some pregnancies, but no babies due to miscarriages and stillbirths. We all hoped that the next generation would survive, otherwise, why were we still here?

My new husband and I had been ordered to start baby-making right away, but nothing had happened yet. I guess he was being considerate, as he could tell that deep down, I didn't want to, but it was our main duty. Sometimes, he pressured me saying,

"I'm not getting any younger, and we need to conceive now while we still can."

I had to move in with him because once you're married, you have to move into your husband's cabin. I wanted to go out on a night-time walk because being out at dark was the only real fresh air we ever got, and it was so refreshing, it reminded you that you're alive, and you were lucky to be alive. The cabin where the Rulers met at night-time was 2 doors down from my new home. It was hard to avoid it now. Anyway, I'll stop writing in this to go for my evening walk. Writing about all this got too much sometimes.

***

I walked alone in the dark as I did most nights, and as I walked past 'The Ruler's' cabin, I stopped and hid behind the wall. I would be killed if anyone found me listening in on their meetings, but I just had to know what was going on. I hated being kept in the dark about the way we will end up living.

'I think we should stick to the first idea. All men and women should live separately. We can't trust human nature. Too many people aren't happy with their new partners, and we can't risk them having any affairs or even speaking to the opposite gender. Husband and wife shall only meet at a certain time when the woman is most fertile, which is when they shall attempt to conceive,' I heard my sister's voice saying.

I continued to hide behind the wall at the risk of being spotted. I had to learn more about this new rule that may come into play at some point soon.

'The plan could work. People won't be happy about it, but we must do all we can to control our next generation. We coupled them up carefully to try and get all types of new babies and risking them having affairs or falling for others is too risky, it could ruin what we have worked for,' Grindon replied, and everyone seemed to agree.

I couldn't believe this. Their leadership was getting out of control. There was no need to control every single baby that would be born, looks and personality just didn't matter as long as there was a next generation to continue our legacy after we were gone.

They were going too far, and I didn't understand why they had to have such unusual rules just to gain more control over all of us. I truly believed that Grindon Hilton was ruthless, and he was doing all of this just so that he could die knowing he rebuilt this town all by himself, and he will ignore all the help he received from the other 4 Rulers.

He masked his strange ideas by convincing everyone that every single decision he made was to help us survive, but how was separating us helping us to survive? I was soon distracted from their discussion as I felt a drop touch my face from up above. I smiled to myself, as I knew the rain had come. It didn't rain very often now, but when it did, it rained for hours. It was good for us because the rain is what kept us alive. We used it to drink and wash with, and so, the fact that it rained for hours at a time meant that it lasted us weeks and sometimes months.

We put buckets down everywhere to collect as much rain as possible. Me and a couple of other people came running over to catch the rain. It was a lot cleaner than before, even though none of us understood why. I placed a bucket in the middle of the street as it began to rain heavily. I saw Kaiser arguing with his new wife just outside of his house that they lived in across the street.

'Please! We need to concentrate on making a family, the pressure is on!' Verona shouted to her new husband as half of the street stared over. Kaiser looked around awkwardly, and he didn't look like he wanted to argue back.

'You don't understand, Verona! You're only 19 years old, it's just so … wrong! I can't!' Kaiser shouted back in her face as the whole town would be able to feel their pain and burdens if they saw this. She shook her head and began to cry slightly, and I just stopped dead and watched.

'I will not die because you're refusing to get me pregnant! You'll end up killing us both!' Verona shouted back as she sighed and slammed the door in his face. Kaiser looked at everyone who was watching, but he noticed me. He gave me a half smile, and I gave him one back, and then we all watched him walk away as we were soaked by the rain.

Watching all of these newly married couples argue over trying to conceive made me realise that there really was no chance of happiness. There was no chance of happiness in a loveless marriage. But when I really thought about it, the option was to have 5 children as soon as possible or be killed for not reproducing. I knew I was capable of having children, as I gave birth to my twin boys at 23 years old. I took the full bucket of water to my cabin and placed it on the floor.

'We have more water. What a miracle,' I said to my husband as he laid on the bed and stared over at me while I placed the bucket on the floor awkwardly. Living with a man that I barely knew did make me feel uneasy. He smiled at me, and then I sat next to him on the bed.

'I don't want to, but maybe it's time that we tried to ... you know,' I suggested, feeling severely out of place.

He looked at me as though he was unsure whether to take me seriously or not. It's not like I would enjoy any of it. I lost my husband three years ago, and the pain was still raw. Laying with another man would be more than disturbing. Bringing a child up in this sort of world was just too much to even imagine. Most people were acting as though all of this was normal because they had grown to accept it, but I never would.

'If you feel the time is right, we might as well get the job done,' Cyrus said to me as he gently placed me onto the bed. As soon as he tried to kiss me, I flinched and looked away.

'No, I'm sorry. I keep messing you around like this, but I need more time,' I said as he looked at me and then got off me.

'Okay, I won't rush you. I didn't exactly want to be remarried either. Not after losing my wife, I never truly got over her death. But we do what we need to survive,' he explained as he sat on the edge of the bed, no longer anywhere near me. Whenever he got too close, I had to get away. I couldn't stand him touching me in any way. Although he did seem like a decent man, I just couldn't imagine being intimate with him.

This marriage was constantly on my mind and how much I didn't want it. To say that I was genetically made, I don't think my thoughts were what the scientists had planned. But nobody would ever know. As I sat and thought about this miserable life once again, I looked over and noticed that Cyrus had fallen asleep, and the night was only getting darker as it was getting later. I laid my head down to rest on the piece of thin cotton that we used as a pillow. He was fast asleep next to me within 10 minutes.

Now that I felt alone, I was filled with a sudden sense of dread and fear. I went ice cold from head to toe, even though it was at least 24 degrees at night. The breeze coming from under the door just wasn't enough to make me cold. My body was unresponsive. I could move my eyes, but I couldn't do anything else, I felt paralysed. There was nothing but darkness in the cabin with only a hint of light coming from just outside, under the door.

My attention fell completely to a dark shadow that emerged from under the door. I focused on it, and I felt my whole body trying to shut down, to give into it. I found the strength to slowly get up out of bed. Maybe I was being pathetic, maybe there was just someone outside the door, and I was determined to find out who. I pretended to be brave, I walked up to the main cabin door and opened it quickly to get it out of the way. As soon as I opened the door, there was nobody there, and the shadow had disappeared.

I felt the presence suddenly behind me instead. As I went to turn around, I saw a flash of bold blackness out of the corner of my eye. I turned around as soon as I saw it, was Cyrus awake? Was he trying to trick me? If he was, it wasn't funny. I looked back at the bed, but he was still fast asleep. Maybe I was just confused and tired. I went in the direction that I thought I saw the shadow heading in, and it led me to a piece of wood that rested on the floor.

I couldn't remember seeing it before. There was some writing carved into the wood that read 'Death is Peace.' I dropped the wood immediately. It made me wonder who would go to all of this effort to intimidate me. I blinked to see if it was still there; I hoped it was exhaustion making me see things. I picked the wood back up again, and I looked on both sides. There was nothing there, and that cold presence that often hung over me had disappeared once again.

Everything felt normal again, and no shadows could be seen. I dropped the piece of wood and stared at it in confusion. Something was going on, there was a greater force trying to influence my life. The only problem was finding out why.

Chapter 4

20th June: 3002

So, a lot has happened since I lost wrote in this. I got so busy and couldn't keep up with it sometimes. I was a month into my loveless marriage, and there was no sign of any improvement. Just a week ago, we did consummate the marriage, even though it felt more like rape because I really didn't want to, but it's that or accepting death. I had accepted that it would never feel like a marriage, but this was my life now.

I had to wait just a few more weeks, and then I would find out whether I was pregnant or not. If I could just show that I was following the rules by doing the deed with my new husband and by getting pregnant, then the Rulers wouldn't have any reason to dislike me or threaten me.

Plus, if I was pregnant, I wouldn't have to have intercourse with him for a while, not at least for another 9 months. Thank goodness we had lost a lot of the technology from before as it would only be around 5 months instead. I can't write in this, not today. I can feel my new husband's eyes all over me. He is probably wondering why I keep writing in a diary, but I don't need to explain myself to him. He doesn't understand that this is the only place I can write my true feelings down without the risk of being killed for speaking out against our new leader. I'll write in here again when he's not around.

***

I put my notebook down and walked out of our shared cabin because I felt so lonely being with someone I barely knew. As I left, I saw a friend that I had made in the first few months. A 31-year-old woman named Erica Westbourne. She greeted me with a smile and a quick hug, even though it was against the rules. No human contact was allowed with anyone except your partner.

'It does get boring around here once you've finished your duty for the day. But I guess we're lucky to be alive. I miss the flying cars and the healthy food that tasted exactly like chocolate, so you could enjoy the taste but only put goodness into your body,' Erica said instead of saying hi. Smiling was a new way of saying hello, so you could get straight into a conversation.

We stood on the path in the middle of our street and had a good chat, at least they couldn't stop us from discussing the old times. I nodded and laughed along, talking with her or one of the other girls was the only real conversation I had. I couldn't even talk to my sister without her connecting it to politics, as she felt that she was so close to the man in charge that nothing else mattered, not even family.

'I miss all of it. But of course, I miss my little family the most. All technology aside, I miss basic freedom and knowing that there's no pressure on us to carry on the human race,' I responded as she looked at me with sympathy and agreed.

'Last year wasn't so bad. Things were starting to improve. We had street parties, and we were all free to do as we pleased. Things just weren't as strict back then. I don't know what changed. Maybe the fact that we all found out that we were dying,' Erica replied as I looked at her and thought about what she said. Erica was then shouted back into her cabin by her husband, so she gave me a quick wave goodbye.

I continued to have a quick walk because apparently, in about an hour, Grindon was giving us the weekly speech. It usually involved any news and new rules. Every single one of us dreaded the speech. It was safe to say that things had become complicated with Kaiser and me. In the last month, we had grown close, and we kept meeting in alleyways and speaking whenever we could. He tried to kiss me, but I backed away. We have admitted to one another that there is a mutual attraction, but of course, nothing can happen; it's too dangerous.

We can only ever be with our match. To have control over my actions, I asked him to try his best to keep his distance. I already felt guilty for even looking at another man after my husband's death. I stared over at his house, as it was just across the road. He was probably all cosy with his 19-year-old ginger wife.

'Flame tornado!' I heard a random woman shout at the top of my street.

It made me jump because I was daydreaming, and then my thoughts were interrupted by the fact that we could all be burnt alive by a burning wind made of flames. The 'Tornado Whistle' went off as Grindon came running out of the Government Cabin and everyone ran to the same area. There wasn't really a safety area because we had no giant brick walls to hide behind or any tables to hide under, but we had to gather together, so Grindon could do a head count and make sure everyone was still here.

I saw Kaiser come running out with his wife, who was half naked. I looked at him with an obvious jealous eye, and then I continued to run to the 'Tornado Point'. As soon as it looked like a lot of people were here, Grindon started counting. I stared over at the tornado. It was like nothing anyone could imagine. It reminded us of the sun mixed with an electrical spark made of fire. I could feel the heat off it even from far away. It came about 4 times a year, and it was so dangerous.

It was just as vicious as any other tornado, but it was made up of fire and wind, making it unstoppable. If it came right in the middle of our town, it would burn down all our cabins and completely ruin our lives. Fire had already done that once, and we hoped it would never happen again. It was about 2 minutes away from our town, as when someone spotted it, it was only in the distance. They moved slower now that they were made of fire as well as wind.

'We're missing 7 people! Everyone keep an eye out!' Grindon shouted, as there was a lot of chatter and panic towering over his voice.

He continued to blow the Tornado Whistle in the hope that the missing 7 people would hear it and come and find us, but the tornado got closer, and there was no sign of anyone else running towards us. Judging by the angle of the tornado, it would only brush our town, and then go in the opposite direction, so there wouldn't be much damage, as long as the people were found. We then saw the 7 missing people running towards us in the distance. They reached out their hands in the hope that someone would risk their own life to grab them away from the tornado.

It was right behind them, and I pushed past everyone and tried to grab the person who was at the back to give them a chance. It was a 13-year-old boy called Codey Jenkins. I wouldn't stand by and watch another young life be taken when it could have been avoided. Everyone stared at me in shock as I ran towards the flame tornado, and I grabbed the boy's hand. The boy was viciously snatched from my hand as he fell into the hell of the tornado and died before my very eyes.

I could only just make out his face when he was sucked into the tornado. I could see the air being sucked from his lungs and the fire burning his remains. We all wished that we still had the weather experts to warn us about things like this. Having no warning got people killed. I stood and stared with tears in my eyes as I watched the tornado come closer to me.

Maybe dying would be the best thing for me, to finally reconnect with my family who I missed dearly. I knew I wouldn't make it if I tried to run back now. I felt myself being thrown to the ground and no longer anywhere near death. I was faced down to the ground as though I had been rescued without wanting to be rescued.

I was then helped up off the floor, and I got up and looked. Kaiser had grabbed me and dived the other way, so I wasn't killed. He risked his own life for mine. Living now was all about sacrifice. Everyone stared at me with their mouths open as though I was a hero to be admired, but I just wanted to do the right thing. Nobody else needed to die.

'Oh my God, are you okay?!' Kaiser asked me in a panicked, over-exaggerated voice as he placed his hands on my cheeks and stared at me, which was too close for the public to see. I removed his hands from my face.

'I'm alive. Thank you,' I replied, looking away to make it look like we weren't as close as we seemed, I did try to hide it well. I saw my sister looking over at me in a suspicious way. I realised that I was a fighter, and even though I was prepared to die for others, I was glad that I was alive. I couldn't help but turn around and look at the damage of the tornado. It was heading in the other direction now, nowhere near Yalford Valley.

All 7 of the people who were trying to run to safety didn't make it. I felt my heart break once again.

Grindon just watched the tornado fade into the distance before he said or did anything.

'We will never forget those lost,' Grindon said as he nodded to some men near him, and they went over to where the tornado hit. They picked up a few badly burnt body parts from the ground and stuffed them into a box. I looked over curiously.

'Where are they taking those? Will they be buried?' I asked Grindon as he just looked at me and sighed. 'That is too much work. They will be disposed of, out of the town, and never seen again,' Grindon replied in a heartless tone. I looked at him and wondered how he could be so cold. There were now only 347 people left on the Earth, and the numbers just kept falling. We all began to separate and scatter around the town now that the tornado threat had gone.

I watched Kaiser's half-naked wife scurry off to their cabin, and then I gently dragged Kaiser into one of the alleyways that were supposed to be out of bounds, but it was the only place that we wouldn't be bothered. He looked at me as though he was wondering why I wanted him on his own, but it wasn't what he thought.

'I need to say something. I can't stay in a loveless marriage; I've tried, and it's a living hell,' I whispered as we stood close in the narrow alleyway. He sighed and looked around to keep watch. He looked quite afraid of something, as though he was holding something back. He leaned in closer to me and began to whisper even quieter than me.

'I don't feel safe in this town. I wish I could just find a new place and live somewhere else. Who knows? Maybe there's other places with conditions like this town. I just ... I keep ... seeing things,' Kaiser said, almost shaking because he was that afraid. I stared at him and suddenly felt intrigued.

'What? What have you seen?' I asked, but then I saw someone walk past the alleyway, and it was too risky, so we rushed out immediately, and I went one way, and he went the other, without answering my question.

I tried to put it to the back of my mind and convinced myself that it was probably just his fear taking over him, darkness was taking over all of us. I took a quick walk to the little fruit shop just outside the town, next to the sign that said 'Yalford Valley welcomes all'. It had an open sign in the window, so I gathered I could go in.

I went in, and I picked up an apple, a pear, and some strawberries, as we had run out at our cabin. Because of the constant warm weather, fruit, and vegetables grew a lot faster. I took them to the man who ran the shop, and I passed him my ration card. We had gone back hundreds of years since the world ended, it was barely recognisable. But since everything was destroyed, we had no choice but to go back to ancient ways of living. It was a massive change for us all.

The bald-headed man who I forgot the name of, looked at my ration card and took away the pear and the strawberries.

'I'm sorry, you only have enough for an apple,' he said as I looked at him blankly. I didn't understand that. I had been saving my points up for weeks, and I just fancied some fresh fruit, which I didn't have very often.

'Why not? I have more than enough points?' I asked the fruit shop owner as he shook his head and passed me the apple and my ration card.

'Josephine's new orders are that everyone can only have one piece of fruit at a time. Anyway, ration cards will be worth nothing soon, Grindon has something new in mind, sorry,' he explained, looking quite guilty for not giving me the fruit that I wanted. I sighed and took the apple.

'Very well, you're only the messenger. Even though I saved up all of these ration points for nothing. There are far too many rules around here,' I replied, biting into my red juicy apple. He shook his head and made me feel like a naughty school child.

'Talk like that will get you killed, missy,' he said, which was strange, and then he leaned in closer to me and continued, 'Death isn't the end, you know. Would it really be so bad to join your husband and sons?' he asked. There was a strange aura about him suddenly.

His deep voice became lighter, and there was a sinister look in his eyes. I stared at him and tried to figure out why he was saying such things.

'Excuse me? I didn't tell you that I was married before, so, how do you know?' I asked, feeling really curious and wondering why he was acting so strange. He didn't normally say much every time I went in.

'Higher powers are upon us. If you sacrifice yourself, you will be greatly rewarded. Into the darkness you go with no looking back, no light, no more sorrow. Follow the shadows, to the valley of spirits,' he carried on, not answering my question.

'What? Please explain what all of this is about. Has someone told you to say this?' I asked as he stared at me, and then his face changed as though he had snapped out of it.

'Is that it or will you require anything else? I'm shutting the shop,' he said, smiling and seeming normal. I just gave him a strange look and left the shop, eating the apple.

***

We were called to the middle of the town that night for Grindon's weekly speech. He would explain all the new rules and shame people if he had to, almost like a verbal warning before death. I gathered around, and I was in the middle this time, not the front. The other 4 members of the Rulers stood behind Grindon almost like a backup, so he wouldn't be the only one who everyone hated.

'We meet here on this night to hear and obey the new rules that will be put into place as soon as they're spoken. From this day onwards, men and women will be separated. Women will take the north and east of the town, while men will take the south and west. Nobody is to speak to the opposite sex unless they're told to by one of the Rulers observe the ladies and let them know when they're most fertile to conceive, and that is the only night you will spend with your husband.' He took a quick breath before continuing.

'You may find this new rule shocking and harsh. But please remember, we are the Rulers of this town for a reason. We have kept every single one of you alive, and you need to trust us. Now, I know there have been a lot of complaints about us pairing you all up, but the idea is that a genetically formed person should marry a natural-born person to see what DNA their baby will have, so we can do some research. But none of this matters as long as we're all still alive,'

Grindon explained as he was interrupted by me, and all the attention was now on me.

'You say you're keeping us all safe, but how can you say that when you have murdered people and tried to justify it? I think it's time we vote for a new government, these rules aren't helping anyone!' I shouted at my own personal risk as some people behind me shouted, 'Yeah!' in agreement. Grindon didn't even reply, he gave me an evil look, and the next thing I knew, I was being dragged away from the speech by two of the Rulers. As I was being dragged off, I saw my sister give me a warning look. I had said too much.

Chapter 5

6th July: 3002

The moon shone over us, and the night darkened. The eerie breeze was carried through our disturbed town.

'We have all been keeping a close eye on you. We have come to the decision that asking too many questions is landing you in deep trouble. So much trouble that if it continues, we will be forced to remove you from our blessed town to prevent further damage,' Grindon said as he sat at his desk made of wood, carved by his own hands, as I stood in the Government Cabin, receiving my lecture.

I looked up at my sister, she didn't seem sympathetic at all, maybe she didn't care if I was murdered just for standing up for our people. She stood behind Grindon with the rest of the Rulers. My sister was getting bigger, as she was pregnant with Grindon's child. There were 4 more months to go, but I had a feeling that she wouldn't be able to give birth because of the amount of radiation. But, of course, if I brought the subject up, it would be dismissed.

I looked at the Rulers and just left. I didn't answer them or argue back. Therefore, the conversation had to end. Their threats wouldn't stop me from standing up for what I believed in. I knew that Kaiser's wife was always out, doing the shopping from 6, so if I went to his cabin now, I'd have some time alone with him in private.

It was always a risk that Verona would come home and find us talking and become suspicious because she always took a different amount of time whenever she went shopping, so it was hard to predict. As soon as I walked into his cabin, his eyes lit up, and he ran up to me and kissed me passionately.

'I've missed you so much! I really can't hold on much longer, I want us to be together properly,'

Kaiser said as he finally let go of me, and we both sat down.

I smiled at him awkwardly and couldn't get over how attracted to him I was. I never thought that I'd look at anyone in that way again after my husband's death.

'Look, I didn't come around here to spend time with you. I came to say that we can't do this anymore. It's too risky, and I've been warned. If I step out of line one more time then they will kill me, I can't avoid it,' I explained, hoping he would understand, and we would still be friends at least. He sighed and looked around the tiny cabin that he called home.

'Last week was amazing. Finally having our way with each other was what we both wanted. It was clear from the start that, at some point, we would give into temptation, but I understand your position. I'm married. So are you, and I won't risk your life just to sleep with you again,' Kaiser replied, taking it better than I imagined. I released a sigh of relief and felt terribly harsh for doing so.

'I guess, in a way, Verona is an attractive woman. It's just she's way too young for me, and there's a massive personality clash, we're always arguing, we just can't get on,' Kaiser continued without me replying.

I looked at him and tried to hide the jealousy as he admitted to liking his wife. I wish I felt the same about Cyrus. Maybe then sex wouldn't be so awkward. I just nodded and let him continue to go on about his lovely young wife.

'We keep trying for a baby because she keeps pressuring me, begging me actually. But so far, no luck. She just won't get pregnant. She has been pregnant before when she was just 15, but she miscarried so for all we know, she could be suffering with fertility issues. But we'll never know now it can't be proven,' Kaiser continued, but I didn't really take in anything he was saying, I was too busy thinking about all of my problems that just seemed to be getting worse. I began to think about my family before all of this. I hadn't told him about them.

'I actually had twin boys before all of this. They were so headstrong for their age; they were bundles of joy. So, I may have some luck and get pregnant again, I know I'm capable,' I said, almost crying at the thought of my babies and how I wasn't there for them at the end of the world when they needed their mother the most.

He looked at me and looked away, was he jealous that I had been married with kids? Or did he just not know what to say? He cleared his throat awkwardly and wouldn't look me in the eyes.

'So, have you had any luck with your new husband?' he asked, sounding more jealous than casual.

'We've only done it twice, actually, but no luck. With the amount of radiation, I doubt anyone will be able to have a baby without severe consequences, and we need a leader who is more understanding and who isn't rushing people or forcing them to be with people,' I said, sounding disappointed and annoyed about our leader. I didn't want to get pregnant to a man I didn't even like, but if I didn't, I knew what would happen.

I was being used as a baby-making machine, and I had no other purpose, that is what this new world had come to. He smiled at me, and then he gently grabbed me and began to kiss me. I was weak when it came to Kaiser. My mind said no, but my heart always won. The kissing soon got faster, and I felt his hand running up my leg.

This was so wrong, but nothing convinced me to stop. I hated my husband, and my life, so why should I deny myself some happiness? As we kissed, we were interrupted by a loud knocking sound on the side of the cabin. We both jumped and looked at each other strangely as the knocking continued.

'That's not coming from the door. It's coming from one of the walls,' Kaiser said. I was glad he could hear it too because I was starting to believe that I was going mad.

Many people would in this world, it was understandable. We both got up and headed towards the sound, it was endless. There was just one loud knock every second. We both slowly walked out of the cabin, and we walked all the way around it, but there was nobody there. There wasn't even anyone out on the street, but the banging continued.

We then saw Verona approaching us from the other end of the street with a basket of food in her hands. Kaiser smiled at her awkwardly, and I turned the other way and began to walk in the other direction to avoid an awkward encounter. I didn't want to speak to the person who got to marry Kaiser.

As Kaiser walked up to Verona and helped her with the food, I sneaked over to their cabin, to the side where the knocking was coming from. I stared at it curiously and realised that the knocking had stopped. I knocked on the outside of the wall twice, but there was no knock after mine. When I knocked on the cabin wall, I realised that it didn't sound as loud as when we heard it, which made me think that this was another strange encounter. As Kaiser and Verona approached the house, I went to walk away, but I noticed some leaves on the floor.

They looked like a trail, so I followed it. I had that feeling again. The feeling of dread and suspense. I didn't feel safe. I followed it, and it led me all the way to where Grindon does his speeches once a week. The leaf trail stopped, and I stared at it for a while and realised that the leaves had formed into letters somehow, but they weren't blowing in the wind like the rest of the leaves.

The leaves said, 'Take the risk, death isn't the end.' I stared at it and processed what it said. It did have some relevance to my life, as I did feel like taking a lot of risks, but I knew it would end in death. Whoever kept leaving these messages knew what I wanted, but I didn't understand how because I hadn't told a soul. I was suddenly distracted by a firm tap on my shoulder. It was cold, and there was a sense of fear that ran through my body. I wondered who it was, so I turned around to see, but there was nobody there. I felt a frozen rush run through my veins, and I shivered, despite being quite warm.

There wasn't even anybody on the street. I walked back to my own cabin and tried to forget what I had just experienced. Maybe if I took their advice, they would stop leaving me messages and trying to scare me. It had to be someone here in Yalford Valley, but there was never anyone around when it happened, and nobody looked suspicious around me, so it became a mystery.

I began to put some new clothes together from old rags and fabric plants, as I believed that my clothes were becoming too worn, and Cyrus needed some more clothes. As a wife, it was my duty to make sure he got them. Cyrus came back just after I got in. I tried to just carry on with the clothing because I only spoke when he spoke to me, we were so different that there just wasn't much to talk about. He sat across from me and just stared into my eyes with desire.

'So, shall we try a few times tonight, as it might be our last chance for a while?' Cyrus asked with awkwardness in his voice that he obviously wanted to hide from me. Who knows? Maybe he wasn't attracted to me either. Maybe there was a mutual repulsion that we both felt too harsh to admit. I looked up at him and put the cloth down to concentrate on the conversation.

'I'm sorry, but I'm not feeling up to it today,' I answered, knowing refusing to get pregnant was probably against the law as well. He shook his head and began to raise his voice straight away, which was unexpected.

'Tomorrow, we will be apart because men and women are being separated, as planned ages ago, so we need to do it tonight to try and conceive!' he shouted back at me as I stood up like I always did when I was becoming emotionally involved in an argument. Things were complicated between me and Cyrus. I felt like I didn't love him or even like him in that way, but whenever we argued, I was always passionate about it, I had no idea why. I also raised my voice as an immediate reaction.

'I know! And I'm sorry, okay! I just ... can't!' I shouted in his face as he looked at me with that dreaded look of his.

'Is this because of Kaiser? I've seen you going to his cabin a lot the last few weeks,' he replied, making me feel incredibly anxious.

'Okay! YES! I'm in love with him!' I shouted, not even knowing I loved him myself. Could I really trust Cyrus with a secret that would get me killed? I hardly knew him.

'No, you can't love him! It's too dangerous! I won't be married to someone who is having an affair, it's always been wrong, and it still is. I'm sorry but you either end it with him, or I will be forced to tell Grindon that you're cheating, and you may even be killed for it. I will not raise another man's child!' Cyrus shouted back at me. I squinted to hold back the tears, as I knew he was right. My own husband was willing to kill me just because I was in love with someone else, but it was obvious that this would never be a proper marriage.

I didn't see the big fascination with having a baby straight away. I wouldn't mind another little soul to bring up, but surely someone must know that the baby will likely be disfigured or deformed because of the radiation levels. It's amazing how much the human body has changed over time. Evolution has its ways.

People no longer had wisdom teeth. Some younger people didn't even have little fingers anymore. Things that were not needed were slowly phased out by evolution. It did make me wonder what the next generation would be like. Would they have better hearing and sight, or would nothing change for another few hundred years?

I wished I could just have a baby with Kaiser, but of course, that wasn't allowed because we had to do whatever Grindon said. He believed that Verona and Kaiser were a better match. If you love someone, you should be allowed to be with them, no matter what. Nobody should be in control of your life, not this much. I think it was time that I stood up for what I believed in, properly this time. My husband had warned me, Grindon had warned me, and my sister had warned me, but it didn't mean I had to listen.

They didn't want me breaking the rules because they knew that people would join my side once they heard my plans for the new world. It would be a better world with much more freedom. I didn't even answer my husband, I just got up and left the cabin. I headed straight for the middle of the town where Grindon gave his speeches, which was where I found the arranged leaves earlier on.

I stood exactly where Grindon had stood. People were walking past and staring over, wondering what I was doing. Nobody ever stood here except Grindon; I would probably be imprisoned just for taking his place.

'There's only so much a human can take, genetically born or not. Did we really survive to be treated like this? Are we really going to stand back and let a man be in charge all because he led a space tour? Yes, he was a space scientist, but that doesn't make him qualified to be our government. We need someone else in power. Grindon Hilton has had 3 years to prove himself, and deep down, we all know his leadership is just getting worse.'

I continued, 'He has paired people up, we have to have 5 or more babies, or we die, and if we break any rules, we die. Tomorrow, men and women will be separated. When will these "rules" end? They aren't saving us; we are alive because we get lucky, not because of his rules. But enough is enough. One man and his four slaves shouldn't be in charge of our lives. If we all stand together, I know that we can make a difference,' I said loudly as people who were walking past ended up stopping and listening.

As soon as I stopped speaking, the people watching began to clap and cheer. Did they like my courage to speak out, or did they agree with me? It was hard to tell, but surely, I'd find out soon. I smiled and looked around at the support I was receiving. I saw my sister staring over. She gave me an evil look and shook her head as though she was signalling that I had crossed a line through body language. I ignored her and carried on smiling at the people who were still clapping.

'You should be our new leader!' a random middle-aged woman shouted over as everyone nodded and continued to clap. Was this my fate? Was I supposed to save the human race and become their leader? Only time would tell, but my voice had definitely been heard.

Chapter 6

19th July: 3002

The murky sky fell over our land and locked us in for the night. Trapped by the darkness, we stayed. The night breeze carried the speech carefully to my ears.

'Separating men and women wasn't an easy decision, but I'd say it's working greatly. We all know our place now, and we are saving the human race by following the rules and...' Grindon said as we all looked at each other with boredom and misery. We had to sit through one of his speeches once a week for the last 3 years. He was rudely interrupted by a man in the middle of the crowd.

'When do we get to vote for a new government?!' the dark-haired man yelled as his friends yelled with him. Grindon bounced his eyes from one person to the next. He dismissed them as soon as they spoke. He was just about to fill their heads with excuses when our attention suddenly turned to something more serious. A woman at the front of the crowd began to cough heavily until her own blood filled the palm of her hand.

We all took a step back and gasped as the only two doctors we had ran over and told us to make some room. *Was she dying?* I wondered. Her eyes began to roll into her head before she began to shake rapidly on the floor. The doctors picked her up immediately and carried her over to 'The Care Cabin', which spanned across three cabins and was set up like a hospital.

Well, as best we could. Everyone stared over as the traditional speech was interrupted by a woman being covered in her own blood and falling unconscious. The panic soon began to spread as everyone tried to get information on what was happening, even though nobody actually knew without an analysis. The Town Bell began to ring by

Grindon, which is how we knew how serious it really was.

'Everyone, to your cabins, now! We will call you all back when we know what is happening!' Grindon shouted as everyone ran to their partners and headed for their cabins. I found Cyrus, and we began to walk to our cabin as more people behind us began to get the same symptoms, and they were carried off to the wooden Care Cabin beds.

'I wonder what all this is about! I have a feeling that it's something to do with those crops in the middle of town because they have been discoloured for two days now!' Cyrus shouted as he paced up and down our cabin. I sat down, as I didn't want to get too worked up over this. I placed my hand on my stomach and then removed it again.

'Let's just hope we have what it takes to survive this, we've come too far for some mystery illness to kill us,' I pleaded, staring out of the plastic window that didn't really work as a window.

Just 15 minutes later, the town bell rang once again, which was a signal for everyone to meet back up for an update. When we got there, the doctor was standing by, ready to speak, not Grindon. I should have known that he would have left it to the professionals to figure out.

'The last thing we want to do is panic everyone, but you all need to be warned. Some of you will remember the deadly effects of 'the Red Flu' from the 2992 outbreak. Well, I'm afraid it has returned. In case anyone doesn't know, it is a fatal flu that attacks the immune system severely. The main symptoms are coughing up blood, seizures, bleeding eyes, blood rashes, and aggressive vomiting. We have 9 cases of it already, and the numbers are quickly going up. It is usually caused by infected ravens and crows, and when their faeces somehow get onto crops that we eat.

The only fruits that we can think of that have looked discoloured are the oranges, bananas, and the ozean fruit. If anyone has eaten any of these fruits within the past week, then you are at a very high risk of developing the Red Flu. It is also contagious sometimes, so please stay away from infected people, as you put yourself at risk. If you develop any of the symptoms, then come to us. Thank you and stay safe,' the doctor said as he went straight back into the Care Cabin to avoid questions.

We all stared as though we were thinking, and we just couldn't believe what was happening. There was a sudden outbreak of the Red Flu, which did sound life-threatening, as if there wasn't enough of that going around already.

I couldn't remember eating any of them. I was more of an apple and strawberry person, luckily. I kept hoping that Kaiser wouldn't get it because I wouldn't be able to stay with him without raising suspicion. Cyrus stared at me, and I knew he was about to ask me something.

'Do you think you're at risk?' he asked as I shook my head and looked at all the ill people who may not make it.

'Right, you 3 come and help us in here. If you put a breathing cloth over your face, there is only a slight risk to yourselves,' one of the doctors said as he pointed to me and 2 other women stood next to me, including my friend, Erica. They both nodded and collected a breathing cloth, which was an invention from 2799. It was used for preventing the spreading of sickness and serious flu.

It allowed you to breathe in and out, but it only let oxygen in and blocked any unknown particles. It was a clever invention that saved lives. Our only inventor, Calvis Briton, a 62-year-old man, only made 10 of them, as he didn't have the material to make any more, therefore, not all of us could be protected from this flu. I did want to help the sick; I always wanted to help others.

I was passed the breathing cloth to put over my face, but I knew it wouldn't grant me full protection. I passed it back to the doctor and then turned around to face Grindon.

'I can't, I refuse to go in there,' I said as everyone looked at me all confused, including my own husband.

'Why the hell not?' Grindon asked aggressively. I sighed and tried to withhold my speech, but I couldn't any longer.

'Because I'm pregnant!' I shouted as my refusal became clear to everyone now. Grindon looked at me, proud, but shocked, as he probably thought I was finally accepting his rules regarding pregnancy. My secret was now out in the open, even though I wanted to keep it to myself until I was further along. Cyrus didn't look pleased with me at all. He gave me that disappointed look, as though he had a feeling that it wasn't his child.

The next thing I knew, Grindon grabbed me and my sister and took us to the smallest cabin that wasn't in use. He locked us in for our safety, as we were the only pregnant women in the town. To be honest, I was surprised that he even cared. I couldn't see Kaiser's face when I shouted that I was pregnant, but I bet it wasn't good. He knew I had to have a baby, but it didn't stop him from being jealous, just like I am jealous of Verona.

Of course, we never admitted it to each other, it was too painful to say. I had no idea if he loved me back, but I wasn't willing to ask him and pressure him. I kept staring through a small crack in the wood to see what was going on outside with the Red Flu. When I turned around, my sister stood almost smiling at me, as though she was proud.

'How far gone are you?' my sister asked me, acting like it was just a casual conversation. I looked down at my stomach and touched it just once.

'I have no idea. About a month, I think,' I replied, looking around the tiny bare cabin as I wondered how long we'd have to stay in here. I felt a difference in her. She was acting like she used to when we got on, before she chose a man over me. I wanted her to be happy, but it was clear that she was only doing all of this for power, not because she loved Grindon.

'I'm so afraid to give birth. I could die, and nobody knows what my baby will look like. You've had kids before, but I haven't,' my sister said, opening up to me for a change. I placed my hand on her shoulder to show support.

'It's not as bad as it sounds, dying in child labour is so rare nowadays. Of course, that was before the world ended. At least we can go through this together,' I replied, hoping she would miss being close to me and choose me.

What I said didn't make Josephine look any more convinced. I hugged her instead, hoping it would feel like it used to.

'Don't worry, sis. We'll both make it, and our kids will grow up together in a better generation than ours,' I said while hugging her. As soon as we stopped hugging, she began to smile. I always found a way to reassure her. Even with how things had gotten between us, she probably didn't want me to reassure her, as she would hate for me to be right.

'I'm sorry to bring this up now, but Grindon has already warned you. If you keep trying to turn people against him privately, he will have to kill you, and I won't be able to save you,' she replied, completely changing the subject. I didn't really know how to react, so I laughed slightly and shook my head to make it look as though I wasn't afraid of death. I wanted to be remembered as the person who died to prove a point, even though I was terrified.

'I'm willing to take the risk,' I answered casually, as though I didn't care about the consequences. Maybe Grindon was only hesitating to kill me because I was related to his new girlfriend.

Casual relationships weren't even allowed for the rest of us, it was engaged or married now. It went awkwardly quiet after my reply, so I peeped through the cracks again. I noticed Kaiser, he was coughing heavily, and then I saw his blood hit the floor. He was alone, his wife wasn't there to help him, and neither was anyone else. I grabbed a sharp pin from my hair and placed it into the lock to release it. I always kept one in my hair, as I didn't trust anyone. As soon as the door opened, I ran out and ran straight up to Kaiser who was helpless on the floor. I grabbed his arm and helped him up, he was so weak and fragile. He looked at me with fear in his eyes.

'What are you doing? It's too dangerous for you out here! I don't want you harming yourself or your baby!' he said as I helped him along to his cabin. I looked at him and smiled.

'Our baby,' I said as he began to stare at me with a mixture of horror and happiness, which I could understand. I helped him at my own personal risk. I saw my sister staring at me through the big crack in the wood, as she hadn't come out of the cabin. I could see that she was wondering why I would risk my life for a stranger.

Of course, he was much more than a stranger, but I was hoping that she didn't know that. Luckily, his cabin was empty, his wife wasn't in as usual. It felt like they were avoiding each other. He continued to cough up blood, so I rushed to clean it up to get rid of the germs and take care of him. I made sure that he always had fresh water to keep himself hydrated. I took care of him as I did my husband years ago. He laid down and stared up at me while I wet his head with a damp cloth to cool him down. It was a dangerous flu, and if not treated properly, it could lead to death.

'I'm really afraid for you. I don't want any harm to come to you. As soon as they find out that the father of your baby is not Cyrus, they will kill us both and maybe even the baby,' he expressed, sounding deeply concerned as any man would. I shook my head and tried to remain strong.

'Yeah, well, they might not even realise that, as you're naturally born, and I am genetically born, it will be the results that they want. As long as the baby makes it, that's all that matters,' I explained as he looked at me with admiration.

'I have a plan, anyway. The people have made me realise that I should be the new leader. By the time our baby arrives, it will be a safe environment for our child to grow up in, as I will be in charge,' I continued as he looked convinced that I was capable of overthrowing the Rulers, including my own sister.

***

By nightfall, 48 people had been infected with the Red Flu, and just two hours after it had spread, 29 of them had died. Their bodies had been disposed of, and the people who still had the Red Flu were being cared for to prevent more deaths. I had been looking after Kaiser for hours now, and I hadn't shown any signs of catching it. Maybe I was just lucky, or maybe it would come at any second. One of the doctors had also fallen ill, meaning there was only one doctor left to take care of us all.

Kaiser was fast asleep, and I was no use to him at the moment. I took a brisk walk down to the Care Cabin to see the patients. I was probably pushing it a bit; I would be told off for leaving the cabin because I was pregnant, and they didn't want to risk me being harmed. As I went in, I recognised everyone who was in there. Then it struck me. Those who had fallen ill were naturally born. The genetically made people hadn't caught the flu, were we immune? I saw Grindon sat in the corner with a breathing cloth over his face, looking terrified. He would only care if he got it.

'You may not believe me, but I have noticed that everyone who has been genetically-made hasn't caught the flu. It might suggest that we have stronger immune systems,' I suggested as he turned his nose up at me and began to whisper to the remaining doctor, as though he was telling him my theory without giving me the credit. I didn't have time for this. People were dying left, right, and centre, and I had to go and check on Kaiser, God knows where his wife had gone.

As I headed towards his cabin, I was distracted by a woman in need. She was almost dead, but she seemed to be struggling. It was horrible to see. I had no idea why she was near an alleyway and not in the

Care Cabin. I knelt down near her and gave her a look of compassion. I didn't know exactly what was killing her, but I could just tell that she was about to meet her maker. She looked about 80 years old. A decent leader wouldn't let anyone die alone, not like this, out in the open and terrified. Her eyes locked on me, but it felt like she was looking straight through my soul. She had to be dying of the Red Flu, maybe her body was too old to cope with it. I went to check her pulse, but she stopped struggling and began to speak.

'Once the darkness comes, there is no turning back. You are halfway there. Welcome the spirits into your life, accept your fate, and defeat the demons to have an eternity of peace. The time is now to stare death in the face. Death is peace. Death isn't the end,' she pleaded in a demonic voice. I hoped that I was hearing things, but I knew it was real.

I stared at her and wondered why she was saying such things, and why the concept of death seemed to be following me around. Maybe I was losing my mind. Maybe this new life was too much for me.

'Sorry, what are you talking about?' I asked calmly. She stared at me, and then her breathing slowed down and finally stopped.

I closed her eyes and hoped that she would rest in peace away from this horrible world. I kept thinking about what she said, but it just never made sense. We had never met before, so if someone had ordered her to say such things to me, then I didn't know what her motive would be. I couldn't think about that right now. My lover was probably near death, I had to be there for him. His wife clearly hadn't been. Maybe she was hiding somewhere to save herself, even though she didn't need to because she was genetically made like me.

I walked past another dark alleyway, which I didn't feel comfortable about because of the previous encounters. I then felt a hand grab my arm firmly and drag me down the alleyway. I gasped and wondered what was going on. This force that I felt had never been aggressive with me before. Of course, it made me panic even more. I realised who it was. It was Edgar Kelton, the third member of the Rulers. He panted and put his dark hood down. I went to speak, but he beat me to it.

'Kalina. I have a message for you from an unknown friend. If you take a risk, you and your child will both die, but death isn't the end. However, if you don't take the risk, then you and your child will live, but be forever in hell,' he said as I stood there looking confused.

Two strange speeches in the space of 5 minutes wasn't good. Edgar's message sounded like a warning, a warning of my nearby future fate. How did people know that I was thinking of taking a risk? He then sneaked back out of the alleyway with his hood up, without an explanation. But he was the only person who had delivered a message that partially made sense to me. I began to walk back to Kaiser's cabin, but I saw Verona head in instead, so I didn't want to take the risk.

I went back to my cabin instead. By the end of the evening, the infection had begun to fade away. We had no idea how it had happened that quickly, but altogether, 44 out of 48 people died. People were always dying in this town, whether it was from radiation, bad weather conditions, mystery flu, or executions. It was clear to me now that death always surrounded us.

Chapter 7

1st August: 3002

Things had really progressed for me. I had my very own campaign, just like the politicians in the old days. People who supported me called themselves 'Kalinists', and my policies were 'Kalinism'. My group was called 'The Kalinas'. I had a feeling that my campaign wouldn't last very long, not with the leader as my rival. He still had some supporters, of course, but most people supported my side. People were constantly turning against Grindon, and I was offering something more civilised.

The Kalinas weren't a very big group. There was just Kaiser, Verona, Erica, Cyrus, and I, so there were 5 of us, which was only one less than the Rulers. As for supporters, I had about 40 so far, which wasn't bad at all. My main policy was freedom and abolishing the death penalty. People were more scared of doing what they wanted because they knew death was the punishment.

People believed that I was brave for giving speeches against Grindon's policies. The only reason that I wasn't dead already was because my supporters threatened to kill Grindon if I suddenly disappeared. Plus, of course, my sister was probably begging him to spare my life in private. Or maybe it was just because I was pregnant, and as soon as I gave birth, he would kill me anyway. Although I didn't always have time to write in this diary, it had become my safe space.

It was incredibly important for me to keep records of everything that happened so that if anything ever did happen to me, people would read my diary and work out that Grindon was responsible.

If I didn't have so many chores and campaign stuff to sort, I would happily sit writing in this all day. But if my enemies found this, they would use it against me. Call me a traitor to The Rulers and kill me whether I was pregnant or not. I had to play my cards close to my chest for my own safety. Plus, I had my baby to protect now. I was playing a very dangerous game, but for the good of what was left of humanity. Anyway, it's time for the washing to be done or people would get suspicious.

***

I was washing some clothes in a tub of rainwater in my cabin, Cyrus sat across from me, just staring. I didn't know whether he was part of my campaign because he felt he had to as my husband, or he just wanted a better leader. Maybe it was that he knew that if I was the leader, he could be with anyone he wanted, and this horrible marriage would be over.

'Tell me honestly. Are you still seeing Kaiser?' He asked me as he stared over with his small beady eyes. I looked up at him and continued to wash the clothes as a distraction.

'I won't lie to you anymore. Yes, I am. Every night, actually, until his young wife gets back. Is that a problem?' I asked, finally telling the truth and not caring, as I felt I had more power these days. He sighed and looked around awkwardly.

'It isn't a problem, as long as you can keep a secret as well,' he responded as he began to pace around the room, and I wondered what he had done to break the law. Was it as bad as me?

Probably not, I was pregnant to someone who wasn't my husband, and the worst part was that I didn't even care. I was in grave danger, but for the first time since the world had changed, I felt like I had control over my life, even if it wouldn't last long. It was a nice change that did give me hope.

'Go on, what is it?' I asked. I hoped he hadn't killed someone or something. He sighed and looked terrified to speak.

He sat back down and looked as though he was about to cry. I waited patiently for his answer.

'I've also been having an affair. It started about two weeks ago. I just at least want us to be honest,' he said, and I did appreciate honesty. I nodded and eventually smiled even though I was in shock. He seemed the loyal type, but there was no attraction, so I did understand.

'Okay, well, thanks for being honest,' I replied as he looked relieved that I wasn't that bothered. I thought to myself that he shouldn't have made a big deal out of my affair if he was doing it himself.

'I'm in love with a man,' he continued as my eyes went wide, and I couldn't believe what I was hearing. The man I had married didn't like me because he was into men. I suddenly came over all nauseous.

Not because he was into the same gender, but because he was forced into a marriage that made him hide who he really was. Granted, it was a much harder secret to keep than mine. Liking the same gender was against every rule of this new world. Anything that wouldn't make a baby was forbidden. But I couldn't refuse to keep his secret when he was keeping mine. He stared at me nervously and waited for a response.

'You're disgusted, aren't you? I can see it in your eyes!' Cyrus yelled. He jumped up and threw his arms up into the air desperately. I warmed his anxieties with a gentle smile.

'No. This is a look of sympathy for you, having to hide your true self and being forced to sleep with a woman. But I feel fear for you. God knows what they'll do to you if you get caught. It's against all of Grindon's policies,' I responded in a particular voice. His face turned to shame and anger. He thought I was attacking him.

'You're in danger too! You have had an affair, and you're pregnant to another man! The only reason you aren't dead is because you are carrying the next generation!' Cyrus continued. I sighed deeply and held my eyes firmly shut for a few seconds.

'Save your energy for the enemy. If I ever get to be in charge, you will be free to be with whoever without having to hide. Just be careful. Neither of us wants this to get out,' I said. I got up and went to walk away to give him some space, but he continued to speak.

'I will raise your child like my own, and nobody needs to know that it's not mine. I won't say anything, if you agree, we can both stay quiet forever,' he said as I looked at him and sighed. I just nodded and walked out and didn't bother to reply.

I had something to do for my campaign. To compete properly with Grindon, I needed to know exactly what he was planning to do next, so I could offer something better. I was to meet with my friend Erica who had agreed to sneak into the government cabin and collect information about a new policy. We overheard them talking the other day, saying that if any babies are born disfigured, there would be no hesitation to kill them. The thought of that made me really worried because my baby was in danger, and I couldn't allow that. I had to do everything I could to make sure it didn't happen.

We walked together until we got to the government cabin.

'Okay, so I need to go in and collect anything that mentions the new policy?' she asked as I looked around to make sure nobody was listening.

'Yes. Anything you can get to prove it, and I'll use it in my speech to convince people why I should be in power,' I said, smirking, hoping my plan would work because it was very risky. Erica volunteered to do this for Kalinism, which I appreciated.

I helped her sneak into the cabin, and then I left her to it, as standing around would raise suspicion. I went to my cabin and waited patiently for about 10 minutes. She said she would meet me back at mine when she had some proof of the new policy. But my thoughts were interrupted when the alarm went off, the alarm that signalled the whole town to meet up immediately. It was the execution alarm when something was very serious, and someone had to be executed straight away.

I ran out of my cabin and ran down to The Stage where the executions took place, and there were loads of people also leaving their homes and running to see what was going on. When I got there, Grindon was standing on The Stage, and my friend Erica was near it, as though she was ready to step on next.

'This woman will be executed immediately! I went to the Government Cabin and found this woman searching for information, and when I asked what she was doing, she didn't answer. Spying on the government is an instant death!' Grindon shouted as I stared in shock, and everyone looked at me because they knew it was something to do with me and my campaign. I saw Erica crying near The Stage. She stepped up and all of my supporters looked horrified as did I.

'Today is the day that I meet my maker. I give myself up to Kalinism, and I will die for it. I do not die in shame, even though I die in fear. Death isn't the end, it can't be. I hope that with my death, Kalina will take over and bring about a better world, one that you will all flourish in. I am willing to lay down my life in order to serve Kalinism and watch it advance before I take my leave of this dark and cruel world. Even though my death is sudden and unexpected, I will not die in vain,' Erica said a memorable speech as we all listened carefully. I was heartbroken. I couldn't believe that collecting information for me had cost a life.

I would never forget Erica, as she had always been a true and loyal friend to me. I couldn't believe she was dying for something that I asked of her, I felt as though her life was being sacrificed just for me to be in power one day. Grindon was so mad with her that he didn't bother doing the ceremony speech. I squirmed when I saw the execution box, I knew what I would have to witness.

My friend would be murdered in front of everyone for simply following my orders. I had never felt this guilty before, and I doubt that feeling would ever go. She kept looking over at me and smiling, as though she wasn't angry with me for getting her killed. Grindon took out the sledgehammer first and then the stick. I closed my eyes and hoped that she would have a quick death.

'Because this traitor's crimes are so bad, she will have her hands and feet broken with this sledgehammer, and then she will be burned to death!' he yelled, but nobody looked impressed, and we all felt her fear. How many more people would die to give me power? She faced death with pure bravery, and she would do it all again just for what is right. Her hands and feet were held firmly down as a man smashed them in with the sledgehammer.

Her scream as she suffered was something I'd never forget, and none of us could do anything about it. We watched her squirm in pain as her hands and feet were broken. She was then tied to the thick wooden pole, just like Prescott Willows was. They then set the bottom of her on fire and watched her burn as though she was a witch from thousands of years ago. We all listened to her scream as she was left to burn to death.

What a horrible death to endure, especially when she broke the law for a very good reason. I felt a sudden turn in my stomach because I was so hurt about what I had to watch. I held my stomach and took deep breaths, hoping the pain would go away. I hoped there was nothing wrong with the baby.

Sometimes, I thought trying to gain power while I was pregnant was probably a bad idea because it was so much stress for the baby. If anything happened that caused a miscarriage, I'd never forgive myself and neither would anyone else. My sister looked over at me, all worried, because I looked as though I was in pain, but I just didn't look at her because she chose to be on her boyfriend's side and not her own sister's.

The screaming stopped, and when I looked up, Erica had passed away, and she was unrecognisable because of all the burns. The pain in my stomach had stopped, but I did worry that I was losing the baby. We were all taken away from The Stage, and we had to go back to work in our cabins for the rest of the night.

***

Late that night, I couldn't sleep. Just the thought of my friend burning alive for a good deed would give me nightmares. So many people had suffered for a better world, and I hoped that one day, it would all be worth it. I lay wide awake while Cyrus laid next to me. I had trouble sleeping before, but now it was much worse. It seemed very cold and dark in our cabin, even though it was supposed to be a hot night like every night.

I noticed a thin shadow in the corner, and at first, I thought I was dreaming, but I eventually realised that I wasn't. I recognised the way the figure was moving. It seemed so familiar. The shadow seemed to be moving in closer, it was intimidating, but the presence wasn't terrifying like what I had felt before.

'Never be afraid of death,' a cold quiet voice called to me. I squinted my eyes a little, and then I realised who it was. My friend Erica had come to visit me. I sat up in my bed without Cyrus waking up. What was I supposed to do?

Was I going mad, or was I being visited by a ghost? She had only just died, maybe I was just in shock. I didn't bother to turn on the light. It may have seemed stupid to deal with this in the dark, but if I returned to reality, she may have disappeared, and I wouldn't have known why she had come to me. I wasn't about to risk that. I panicked. I didn't know what to say or how to react.

'Erica? Is that really you?' I asked, which was probably a stupid question. The next thing I knew, she floated to the bottom of my bed and sat down, the bed moved, which made it even more real. None of it felt real. I could tell that it was Erica, but she seemed so pale and worn. She was transparent, but also very realistic. I tried to ignore the fact that this was a supernatural experience and tried to just remain calm and see what she wanted. Surely there was a reason why she was visiting me.

She smiled even though it looked like a fake smile. Nobody would be happy to be dead, especially the way she had died.

'You need to take over Yalford Valley before Grindon ruins everything,' she gasped, hoping I would hear her and do something. I thought about what she said, maybe it was time that I did something to try and gain more power. I had my own campaign, and I had a lot of supporters; I didn't have anything to lose. The only thing I had to lose was my life.

'You know, I keep getting messages that say death isn't the end, but if I do take over, will I end up dead? Because if I do, what's the point in me taking over?' I asked, sitting up. I kept looking over at Cyrus to make sure he wasn't awake. He kept fidgeting, which made me afraid that he would wake up.

'Just trust me, and the signs you need to...' Erica tried to tell me something, but Cyrus suddenly woke up and turned the solar panel light on. He rubbed his eyes and looked around the room.

'Were you talking to someone?' he asked, confused and still half asleep.

I looked around, but I felt mad because Erica was nowhere to be seen. I looked in every space in the room, but the shadow had disappeared. I sighed with slight relief in the hope that it was just a dream. Of course, ghosts weren't real.

'Err, no, you must have been dreaming,' I said awkwardly as I turned the other way and tried my best to fall asleep, even though I doubt it would have happened. He turned the light off and went back to sleep.

I stared around the dark room and wondered if I was dreaming, or if I would see Erica again. Whether it was a dream or not, I would definitely consider all the information it provided. Something or someone was trying to tell me something, it felt important, but I still wasn't completely clear on the message. However, one thing was for certain. I would plot to kill Grindon to eliminate him once and for all. I would have asked Kaiser to kill him while I distracted everyone with an inspirational speech. If the other Rulers didn't accept defeat, then they would have to die too.

Chapter 8

3rd August: 3002

It was the time of the week for Grindon to make his speech in front of the whole town. But I had beaten him to it. I would give my speech about freedom and not care that I was taking his place. It was on this very night that we planned for Grindon to be killed. If the Rulers tried to take over after his death, then they would have to be killed as well. Everything had been carefully planned over the past 2 days, and I believed all of it would work. If it didn't, we would die for planning it.

'As we all stand here today, we think of what life used to be. Mistakes were made to make the Earth so bad that global warming almost wiped humanity out completely. And yet we are forced to witness survivors, such as ourselves, being murdered for not obeying every demand from the Rulers. If you choose to join Kalinism, you choose freedom. No more having to hide who you really are. No more having your romantic partners chosen for you. No more death penalty. Just surviving together in harmony. Just peace while welcoming the next generation. Join us now, and this awful reality that we are forced to live in everyday will be nothing but a distant memory,' I said as people gathered in front of me and looked so inspired by what they heard.

As I spoke, I looked over at Kaiser to make sure he was in position. He was hiding behind a wall, spying on Grindon and the other Rulers. Everyone but my sister was there. Grindon and the Rulers were walking just in front of where Kaiser was hiding, but they hadn't noticed him because of his disguise. I kept talking to keep everyone distracted, but I kept looking over at Kaiser to make sure everything was going according to plan. I saw him reach for the knife in his pocket. I suddenly saw my sister just behind Kaiser as though she was walking up to Grindon. She screamed slightly and stepped back.

'Grindon, look out! He's got a knife!' She yelled as everyone screamed and ran around in a panic. Two members of the Rulers grabbed Grindon and threw him down to the ground to protect him.

I stared over in horror, knowing that our plan had been ruined by my own sister. I then saw Grindon as he was helped up off the floor. He brushed the dirt from his clothes lightly, and he began to pant heavily with shock.

'Arrest him!' He shouted as Kaiser was then grabbed by 3 men. Grindon then looked over at me as he could tell how heartbroken I was over Kaiser's arrest. It probably looked suspicious.

'He's part of Kalina's campaign, her speech was a distraction for my assassination attempt! Arrest her as well!' Grindon yelled as people came running over and tied me up ready to be arrested.

We were both sent away to a cell, which was basically a tiny cabin that was locked and only the Rulers could tend to us and visit us. I was left to rot in my cell room until the door opened, and I saw Grindon walk in. Maybe he was about to kill me straight away because he thought I didn't even deserve to die in public.

Or maybe he was about to tell me that my lover would die before me, just so I could watch, he was that cruel. He came and sat across from me, smirking.

'I suspected that you and Kaiser were more than just good friends. If that baby in your womb is his, then I have no reason to keep you alive any longer. There's no reason why he or anyone else should suffer for what you have clearly set up. So, I'll make you a deal. If you admit that you were behind the assassination attempt, then I will spare Kaiser's life, and all of this will be over,' Grindon explained as I listened carefully and sighed towards the end of his sentence.

I did feel relieved that Kaiser would be spared. I couldn't bear to lose him for something I had asked of him. I nodded, even though it was painful to agree to.

'I will admit it if you spare my life. I know you want me dead, but my baby needs to survive. Your words, not mine,' I responded, hoping to at least be killed after my baby was born. He sighed and gave me an evil look.

'I don't care. You shouldn't have broken the rules. You put your own child's life at risk by trying to overthrow me in such a radical way. Plus, in the past few weeks, 5 more women have become pregnant, so the baby of a traitor is no longer required. We have no reason to keep you alive. You will be executed tomorrow night. There is no getting out of this Kalina, you have been defeated, and you will die for trying to overthrow me,' Grindon explained as I felt terrified knowing the life of my child was about to be sacrificed.

Before I had the chance to beg for my child's life, he got up and left me in my cell alone. As soon as he left, I burst into tears. Death was daunting enough without thinking about the fact that my baby would die as well. Maybe I would die easier knowing my baby was alive and safe, but that was impossible. I was only 3 weeks pregnant; the baby hadn't had the chance to develop properly. I didn't know whether that was a good or a bad thing.

My sister would get to live a long and happy life with her new baby even after everything she had done, yet I was going to die tomorrow, and my baby had to die as well. In the old world, politicians accepted competition and slaughtering opponents was against the law. As I laid and cried alone in my cell, I began to think about how much I had tried to take power.

I kept thinking about how I was dying for a good cause, and at least I had tried, because if I hadn't, I'd be stuck in this world without knowing if I could have done something. I would be annoyed to die, knowing that I never had the chance to be in power and show everyone how much the world would change.

But at least I did something. I watched people suffer and did nothing, but I eventually had the courage to stand up for everyone. Maybe people would remember me as the person who took a chance and died for them. I would die for peace and freedom and for a better leader. I couldn't help but wonder whether my first husband would be proud of me for all that I have achieved and risked, or would he be angry that my foolishness had cost me my life?

I then suddenly felt a familiar presence, one that I recalled used to make me feel calm and safe. One that I hadn't felt in years. It seemed I was no longer alone. I slowly turned my head to the other side of the cell, and I focused on what my eyes were telling me. I tried to familiarise myself with the shadow that was before me. I smiled to myself and almost cried with happiness.

'Roman? Is that you?' I asked as the shadow continued to move closer. The face started to form, and I recognised who it was. My husband had come to visit me before I died. He smiled at me brightly and came and sat next to me, and it felt so strange to see him again. I had to force myself to get used to not being with him.

'Kalina. I am so proud of you,' Roman told me as he placed his hand on my cheek and then hugged me tightly, even though it didn't feel very tight, as he was just a spirit in reality. I began to cry heavily as I thought of my death tomorrow and how there was no way out of it.

I always felt free to show my emotions in front of Roman. He held me as I cried, just as he used to, and it always made me feel a lot better.

'Death isn't as bad as you're thinking. I've never been this happy, and soon you will be reunited with me and our sons,' he told me as I smiled at the thought of being with my true family once again. I felt his grip loosening, and his spirit was beginning to fade.

'I have to go now; my time is running out, but we will be together sooner than you think. I love you,' Roman said as he disappeared into the passing dust, and I was alone once again. I laid down on my bed in the cell and cried as I thought about my death.

It did bring me some comfort to know that I had been visited by my husband, whether it was real or not, I needed it to carry on. I kept thinking about being with my family, and it helped me cope with the fact that I would die tomorrow. I got so tired of crying and fell asleep.

THE NEXT DAY

Well, this will be my last ever diary entry. I just hope that one day, someone finds this and reads it. I'm surprised I was allowed my notebook in here. For a full day, I had waited to die in my cell. I was given rotten fruit to eat, and I was treated like a common criminal, even though the risks I took were to gain a better life for everyone. I would give a speech right before my death to say my piece before I left. I doubted that everyone agreed with my death, especially my supporters and my campaign.

I was told this morning that my sister had begged Grindon to show me "mercy" by giving me a quick death and not one full of torture. I couldn't understand why she couldn't convince Grindon to let me live, it felt like she didn't care for me at all anymore.

Power was more important to her. The time had come for my death, 9 p.m. on the 4th of August 3002. They would come in and drag me out any second now. I suppose I should be grateful for not being tortured to death while pregnant, but Grindon was an evil dictator. Couldn't my supporters stage an uprising and somehow stop him?

Were people really going to stand by and watch a pregnant woman be killed? I was scared, of course I was. But I felt a deep shame for not succeeding in my attempts to overthrow him. It seemed ridiculous to keep giving people the death penalty like this when there weren't many of us left in the first place. Kaiser was smart. Maybe when I died and it was over, he would get his revenge on Grindon and find a better way to take charge. I should have known to plan better. But there was no point in regrets now.

I guess this is it. I can hear the jailer's footsteps getting closer, it's my time to go. If you are reading this, I hope the world has become a much better place for you. I hope the awful things I have endured will go down in history so that nobody ever repeats them again. Humans never learn from wars or dictatorships, do they? It's a real shame. We had a chance to start a brand-new world when the ozone layer blew up, but we have fallen into the same habits. Well, goodbye world.

***

I quickly buried my notebook in a space below the wooden desk, hoping someone would find it in the future. I was then roughly escorted to The Stage where my life would end. It had been a long life full of pain, but I was glad that in a way, my death had meaning. I was dying for a greater cause. Everyone was waiting to see me die; it felt like something from my worst nightmares. I could never have imagined this. Grindon stepped onto The Stage, and I walked on after him, trying not to think about the pain of my own death. There were many people gathered around, but the only faces I really noticed were that of Kaiser and Josephine. They were both crying slightly, even though they were trying to hide it. I always thought that I would die for carrying Kaiser's baby, not for trying to assassinate the main Ruler. I stared around and prepared myself for my final speech, and of course, I had tears in my eyes. I was more devastated about my unborn child never getting a chance to live than losing my own life.

'So, this is it. The end has come for me. But it doesn't mean it's the end for you. To all my supporters, carry on standing up for Kalinism. Just because I will be gone from this world, it doesn't mean that you have to suffer as well. This world can be a better place, you just need to make it happen. I make Kaiser the head of my campaign because I believe he will continue in my footsteps and make sure that the world becomes what I spoke of it. Some may say that trying to assassinate a member of the Rulers was wrong. And murder is wrong no matter the reason why. But I did what I had to do, for us to prosper.'

I searched the crowds with my dying eyes and continued, 'I failed, and now I'm paying the price. Maybe this is fate's way of saying that I was never supposed to be the leader, but someday, a new leader will take over. A better one. One that you can all rely on, an honest and fair leader, not one that makes death legal. I hope I will be the last of us to die, and I die today for my people and Earth, not me. I say my final goodbye to you all.'

I wiped the tears from my eyes and tried to see what good I had done at the end. 'These 3 years have been an honour to spend with you as the last survivors on Earth. May peace finally find you. Goodnight world,' I said with powerful passionate words as I tried to put on a brave face to keep my dignity in my final moments. I heard the clashing of the execution box against the wood that made up The Stage. I took a deep breath, as I knew that my death was slowly creeping up to me. I had seen the signs for a while now telling me that 'death wasn't as bad as I thought' and 'death was peace'. But it wouldn't stop the fear that was running through my veins. Everyone was afraid of death, whether it brought us peace or not. The fact that there would be nothing once I died was the worst part to come to terms with. I wanted to truly believe that I would be with my husband and my sons, but a part of me didn't believe in the afterlife or heaven, as many people did thousands of years ago.

I could see out of the corner of my eye that the sledgehammer was being removed. I would get a few quick blows to the head to end my life quicker. My sister sobbed as soon as she saw the weapon, but she had played a part in my death just as much as Grindon. I smiled quickly at Kaiser to try to make him feel like I wasn't scared, but he looked angrier. I knelt down onto my knees, ready to have my life taken from me, and die knowing my baby would die too. I closed my eyes and took another deep breath, but I was distracted.

'No!' Kaiser shouted as he tried to push past the Rulers' bodyguards to get to me. I looked up and smiled at him romantically. It was sweet that he couldn't bear to see me die, and he wanted to rescue me at the last minute. I was glad that he wasn't going to be killed as well. I could tell that he wanted to get to me and stop the execution, but that would be impossible. They'd find a way to kill me either way.

'You can't do this! You can't kill our baby and an innocent woman, it's wrong!' Kaiser yelled. Everyone looked at us as though our affair was the best gossip they'd ever heard. But with one look from me, he knew that he couldn't save us. He finally stopped trying to push past the guards, and he silently cried while staring over at me.

Grindon stepped back and got ready to kill me with his own hands. I paced myself to meet my end. This was the most afraid I had ever been in my life. But I was ready to take all of the pain just for my cause and my campaign, hoping that one day, I would have died for a good enough reason. As soon as I saw the sledgehammer being raised, I turned and looked at Grindon.

'You are a weak killer for murdering an unborn child. May hell find you,' I whispered to him. I could tell that there was a part of him that felt afraid. He knew I meant every word when he looked into my eyes. He soon ignored me and continued to practise swinging motions with the sledgehammer. He didn't normally do this. He was either dragging it out to make me suffer even more, or he was ordered by my sister to make sure it was one clean swing that would kill me straight out to make it less painful.

The moon was hanging over our land like a lamp used to light up a morgue. The breeze was cold and frightening. The crows were cawing and daring to look through to my damned soul. The smell of flesh, blood, and tears took over my senses as I stood in the place where many others had died before me. I never thought I would have died this way. I used to believe myself to be too sensible to do anything that would cause me to get the death penalty. The wooden floor of The Stage was still heavily stained with blood, and my blood would soon join it. I heard the clanging of metal creeping closer to me, ringing in my ears.

I was supposed to protect my baby, not get us both killed in an attempt to take over. Why was it so important for me to take over anyway? It all seemed pathetic, as though I was about to die for nothing. Memories of what my life used to be like flashed in my mind's eye, reminding me of what I had lost in my lifetime. Nothing would be as painful as losing my whole family. Then, I knew it was almost over. I felt the steel brush my neck, going deeper and deeper into my flesh.

There was just no pain like it. The pain felt like pressure in my skull. Then my eyesight began to blur, and I felt my whole-body collapse. As I laid on the blood-stained wood of The Stage, I waited impatiently to meet my end. It seemed that one clean blow of the sledgehammer had stunned me, but not killed me. I looked at the crowd for a split second until my vision went completely, and I felt the force hit me once again.

I steadily took my last breath as I felt my brain being exposed to the air around me. I felt blood pouring from my head as my body and senses grew weaker. I could feel myself slipping away. The last thing I managed to do was place my weak hand onto my stomach one last time. Then, I took my leave of the world. And what a rotten world it had become.

I followed the light until I got to the end of the tunnel. They were there, greeting me with the happiest smile I had ever seen. The children were so full of joy, and Roman was too. I looked around me and there was nothing but bright lights. The Earth was back to the way it was before, the way we all loved it. My sons grabbed my hands, and we ran away into the distance, playing tag as we always did. We stopped and admired the great waterfall, and butterflies of all colours glistened in the sun.

The birds were singing lullabies, and the blossom trees were gently waving in the breeze as the blossoms fell and hit the lake without a sound. I felt nothing but love and safety. I could smell nothing but fresh water, nature, and trees. I could see nothing but beautiful scenery and my family. I was free. Death had set me free.

Chapter 9

21 YEARS AGO

'Now that I'm 16, I have to leave this science lab. I have been told to get a proper job to earn money for myself. I am afraid because I've got no experience in being in the outdoor world. Everyone looks at me like I'm a monster. They're so judgemental. I'm only telling you all of this, so you have 3 years to prepare yourself for when you turn 16 and this happens to you as well. You will have to leave this lab, your home and work, instead of helping scientific research,' Josephine explained to her younger sister, Kalina, as they both sat in one of the spare rooms of the lab that they were born in. Kalina stared at her and tried to imagine what it was like in the real world.

'The world is cruel to those who are genetically-made. People often belittle me in my new job because they see me as some sort of monster just because I wasn't carried in a womb,' Josephine told Kalina as Kalina stared back at her in horror.

'It all sounds terrifying. Will we … die?' Kalina asked, staring around with a look of terror on her face. Josephine placed her hand on her sister's cheek and smiled for reassurance.

'You're my little sister. I will always protect you, no matter what. I won't ever let anyone hurt you, I promise,' Josephine replied, putting a smile back on her sister's face, but it didn't last very long.

'Josephine? Life goes so quick. Is there a life after death?' the young, curious Kalina asked her older sister with some hope in her voice. Josephine laughed and looked the other way.

'Don't believe such stupid rumours. When you die, that's it. There's just nothing. But when you do die, don't show you're afraid, it will ruin your reputation. Being remembered as brave near the end is the best way to go,' Josephine said. Kalina never got that out of her mind, not ever.

***

My eyesight slowly returned, but I couldn't understand how. I squinted and looked around me, all dazed but in a bit of a panic. I looked down to find myself floating. I was floating, even though I was meant to be lying down. I began to recognise people around me. Neighbours, family members, friends. In the distance, there was a rainbow, and there was plenty of green land and peaceful blue water. Something that I had never seen, even before the world blew up. I couldn't understand why I was somewhere when I was dead. Had I survived?

'I thought I was dead,' I said to myself as my voice echoed strangely. Wherever I was, it looked magical.

'We've been expecting you,' a familiar voice said as I turned around and realised that my oldest friend, Crystal Stewart, was standing smiling at me. She was dressed all in white, and I realised, so was I. Everyone in my sight stared back at me and smiled. It looked so heavenly.

'Crystal? You died with everyone else. What is going on?' I asked, wondering how I ended up in this magical place that I had never seen before. The strangest thing was that it was nice and bright, but I wasn't burning from the radiation, none of this made sense.

My old friend hooked into me, and we started walking together.

'Welcome to the after world. A place of peace and life after death. Death isn't the end as you can see,' Crystal told me as I stared at her and wondered if this was just a dream, my death and waking up here. None of it seemed believable. People often spoke of heaven and the afterlife, but I didn't think at any point that it was real. It was near impossible in my opinion. A part of me hoped that my death was just a dream, and so was this, and at some point, I would wake and realise that I still had a chance of being Yalford Valley's leader. I continued to look confused and expressed that I didn't understand anything that was being said.

'None of this is real. It can't be,' I exclaimed as we continued to walk, and all I saw were waterfalls, flowers in full bloom, clouds, and a rainbow. It was a sight that people had only spoken about but never had the privilege of seeing. Whether this was a dream or not, I would remember this forever.

'I understand your confusion. None of this was easy to accept for any of us. But I will prove to you that the after world is real, and this is not a dream,' Crystal said as we stopped in the middle of nowhere, and even though I was walking, I couldn't feel my feet touch the ground. She then stretched her arm out and went to touch my hand, but I felt nothing. I looked down, and her hand went straight through mine. I was merely a soul with no body. I gasped and pulled away. She smiled and laughed slightly.

'We all had that reaction at first, but you get used to it. We're glad that you took notice of all the signs we kept leaving you. It was worth dying for, and as you can see, death is peace, and it's far from the end,' Crystal continued as I carried on looking around and to see if I could make sense of any of this. It all made sense now. I wasn't going crazy. All the things I kept seeing and the messages left for me, they were all sent by people in the after world. They wanted me to die to come and join them.

But why? Was I in heaven, or was this a mysterious world that only the dead knew about? I smiled at Crystal in the hope that she would guide me and explain in more detail what this place was. I was right, she did.

'You will be happy here, there is no sadness or evil in this world. It's the ideal world that everyone who is alive wishes for one day. Only the kindest souls are sent here after death,' she explained as I tried to get my head around it all. Was this it forever, or would I finally be put to rest eventually? 'There are no negative emotions here or pain. It will feel unusual, but you will be the happiest you've ever been. I wanted to greet you, but other people wanted to see you,' Crystal said as she began to smile, and then she stopped and looked over her shoulder.

I looked in the same direction as Crystal to see what was happening. I saw Roman and my two twin sons stood smiling at me. My husband came running up to me and threw his arms around me as my kids waited patiently behind him.

'This really must be heaven to see you three again, how wonderful! Roman? Is this real?' I asked, as I wasn't sure whether Roman's last visit in my cell was real or not. He put both of his hands on my face, even though they went straight through, but I could imagine his touch.

'It's real enough for me,' Roman replied. I couldn't help but smile. Crystal was right. I could feel the happiness, but I couldn't feel anything else. The pain of my death, the loss of my baby, or my worry for Kaiser. All the bad feelings had disappeared, so it must have been real. It felt like a second chance. Even though I wasn't alive, I felt lucky to have some sort of conscience. My sister was wrong all along.

There was a life after death, and she would never get to witness it because only the kindest people came here, and she was far from that. I did expect a lot more from my older sister. I stared down at my sons, and I thought about how amazing it was to see them again. They looked so happy and healthy, what more could a woman wish for? I couldn't help but continue to admire everything that was around me. The scenery was so beautiful. Crystal then walked back up to us, smiling, with her hands behind her back.

'This world is different for everyone. You will see what you truly believe is beautiful, but we all see something different. I see a beautiful tropical forest. What do you see?' Crystal asked as I was amazed with what I heard. The fact that the world was whatever you wanted it to be was astonishing. I looked around with a smile as bright as the scenery.

'I can see the sun beaming down on me like never before. There is a large rainbow in the distance, and just over there, there is a waterfall and lots of clouds. It looks magical. But why am I really here?' I asked, thinking there was another reason why I was here and not just because I had a good heart. Crystal sighed and looked around, but she still looked happy. Because of all the hurt in the real world, I wasn't used to seeing everyone happy without any troubles.

'This is a place where people stay if they have unfinished business. If you're a good person and you were wrongly killed, or if you died before doing something important, then you'll stay here. Your husband is still here because he keeps haunting Yalford Valley to check up on the people. I'm still here because I wanted to introduce you to this new world. You're here because it is your job to make sure that Kaiser takes over as the new leader,' Crystal explained as I thought about what was expected of me. I went to reply, but Crystal continued to speak.

'All you have to do is close your eyes and imagine where you want to be. When you open them, you will be there,' she continued. It sounded impossible, but so was everything about this place. I felt I had to try it. I did as she said. I closed my eyes and imagined Kaiser's cabin and the room that he slept in, as I knew he would probably be in there at this time.

When I opened my eyes, I was standing in the corner of Kaiser's room, and he was laid in bed, sobbing, alone. His wife wasn't next to him. Possibly because of our affair. It was really dark, and I doubted he would have been able to see me. It felt so strange visiting someone who was alive, but I couldn't feel the sadness. I tried to think about how I would get Kaiser's attention without startling him. I walked closer to his bed, and then sat at the other side of the bed. He suddenly sat up and looked around. Maybe he sensed a presence, as I used to when I was visited by spirits. He turned around to face me. I couldn't tell whether he was happy to see me or afraid.

'You're here. I hoped you would come. I need your guidance. I've missed you,' he said to me, even though I didn't know whether he could see me or just my shadow. He didn't seem scared at all now. 'You have been so brave to take my place. You just need to trust yourself. If you really think, you'll realise that you don't need my guidance at all. Carry on in my name and take over as the new leader,' I said, my voice jittering and echoing. I couldn't get used to being a ghostly presence. He stared back at me and tried his best not to cry.

'I have a plan to get rid of Grindon. It will work this time. Tomorrow night when Grindon is in his bed asleep, and he feels safe, I will go into his cabin and kill him in his sleep. He doesn't realise how vulnerable he is without any of his guards or companions,' Kaiser explained to me, and it did sound like a good plan, one that could work without doubt. I smiled back at him to show him how proud I was. Whether I was dead or not, I wanted Yalford Valley to be run by someone who would be fair and not just kill people for committing minor crimes.

'I will watch over you, and I will be so proud to see you take over,' I explained. I couldn't stop smiling. I really didn't die for no reason. I wasn't happy to be dead, of course, but knowing I could come back and see Kaiser was better than I expected. I could see that he missed me dearly, and he was struggling without me.

I stood up from Kaiser's bed, and I turned around and walked the other way. I faded into the nearby distance as I closed my eyes. When I opened them again, I was back in the after world, and not the land of the living. I looked around and saw my family again. I was so happy to be reunited with them finally. Knowing that they died in pain without me always haunted me, but now I could be by their side for as long as I wanted. I then saw Roman walking up to me, still smiling and happy to see me.

'I was proud of everything that you achieved in your final days. I know you are probably wondering why I'm not angry about you and Kaiser, but as you know, I can't feel anger, so it's all good. You had to move on at some point. All that matters is you are here where you belong. The main thing is whether you believe Kaiser's plan to take over will work?' Roman asked me, as I looked hopeful about the overthrow that would apparently happen tomorrow.

'I have every faith in Kaiser. He has always had the same views as me. I know that if he really tries, he can take down Grindon and kill him. When my business is done, and I want to be finally at rest, will you come with me? So, we can rest together forever?' I asked as he looked at me for a moment before replying.

'Of course, I will. We will all be together again. All you have to do is make sure Kaiser takes over, and then you will be put to rest as there is nothing else that needs to be done,' my husband explained as we stood side by side and stared at the scenery. I stood and thought about tomorrow as I hoped that Kaiser would take over. I felt no sadness. I was finally at peace.

Chapter 10

4th August: 3002

The time had come for Grindon's death. Kaiser planned to kill him by himself, so he could take over. As soon as Grindon was dead, Kaiser would immediately become the leader, as he had the most votes, even the other Rulers couldn't take over, as my campaign had the most votes. I hoped that me and Kaiser would kill Grindon together and then lead the village together with me being alive. I couldn't have that now, as I was among the dead and not the living, but my only goal before I was laid to rest forever was to make sure that I was leaving Yalford Valley in good hands with a better-than-decent leader.

I had no idea how things were with Kaiser and his young wife, but I hoped that he would find happiness again now that I was gone. I was surprised that Kaiser wasn't afraid when he saw me as a ghost, a lot of people didn't believe in ghosts or another world after death, but luckily, he was very open, and he believed what he saw.

Tonight may have been my last chance to see Kaiser, so I wanted to make sure that he took over easily, and I could leave him knowing nothing else needed to be done. I had been walking around all day and admiring the scenery. I had also spent a lot of time talking to my husband about how it felt to live life without him and how alone I felt when he passed away. He said he was constantly seeing me, and he noticed how much I struggled.

I closed my eyes and imagined Kaiser because I knew that would take me to wherever he was right now. When I opened my eyes, I was inside Grindon's private cabin. I saw him laid in his bed, alone. My sister wasn't next to him as she used to be all the time. I hoped that one day she would see what kind of a man he really was and regret siding with him over me. She played a part in my death, and I would never forget it or forgive her for it, even if she begged me.

I saw Kaiser sneaking up to Grindon while he slept. People said that Grindon was always a deep sleeper, which hopefully meant that he wouldn't wake while Kaiser was trying to end his life. After the assassination attempt, I would have thought that he would never dare to be alone again. Kaiser looked over his shoulder to where I was standing, but I didn't want myself to be seen, as it would have probably distracted him from what he needed to do. I saw Kaiser pick up the pillow, and I turned away, as I didn't want to watch the death of someone else.

It was good to know that Grindon wouldn't end up in the after world like me; it was only for good hearts, so I would never have to see him again. Once I heard Grindon taking his last breath, I looked again to make sure that he was dead. I heard Kaiser sigh with relief as he put the pillow back in place. I had always imagined that Grindon would have met his end in a more violent way, like I had to. I heard noises coming from outside of Grindon's cabin.

They always said that the dead have better senses than the living. Kaiser didn't react to what I heard, which led me to believe that he was unaware that there were people outside. As he went to walk out of the cabin, I could hear someone approaching on the other side of the door.

'There is someone out there. You aren't safe yet,' I whispered to Kaiser as he soon realised that I was there, and he wasn't just imagining it. The door then burst open, and two of Grindon's guards walked in.

'He's killed the leader! We need to end him before he can take over!' one of the guards shouted as I stared in panic. I couldn't really feel the panic, as I no longer had feelings, but if I was alive, I would have been panicking then. He looked at them with fear as he realised that taking over would never be that easy. Kaiser looked around in a panic.

He soon noticed Grindon's knife by his bed. He reached for it. The next thing I saw was the guards running toward Kaiser. I watched closely as Kaiser fought them off. He stabbed the guards but didn't kill them. They fell to the floor hopelessly. I smiled, as I was proud to see him stick up for himself and his new power over the valley. It was great that he didn't want to kill anyone.

Kaiser then rushed out of the cabin and walked off, trying to act normal, so he didn't look suspicious. Because Grindon's door was wide open, and a random man went running in. Just a couple of seconds later, he came running back out again.

'Everyone! Our leader, Grindon, is dead. I cannot tell what he died of. But we must go by the votes and say that Kaiser is now our new leader!' the man shouted as Kaiser stopped in the street and looked back at him, and most of the people began to clap and cheer.

I hid in the alleyway and watched them cheer. I was so proud of him. Even though I was dead, I did feel as though my death had a part in Kaiser taking over, which meant it was worth my life. I then saw Kaiser walk onto The Stage as everyone spread the word and began to gather around, ready for the new leader's first ever speech.

'So, we now know that our previous leader, Grindon, has been pronounced dead, and as the second in command for Kalinism, I must take over. Nobody knows how he died but finding out isn't at the top of my list. We have more pressing matters.'

He continued, 'Kalina died for nothing. Many other innocents died before her for nothing. That stops now. No more pointless deaths. I will not stand by and watch more of us being sacrificed, especially when there aren't many of us left. All of Grindon's policies are erased. You can all be with whom you choose. There will be no more of the death penalty, and I will not force any of you to have a child just to help the population. May happiness finally find us,' Kaiser said as everyone clapped and cheered. It was an amazing speech, and I knew that the minute he took over, he would make the world a better place. He smiled and looked around at his people.

'Tomorrow, there will be a proper funeral for everyone who was unjustly killed by Grindon, including Kalina,' Kaiser announced as I smiled because I was finally having a funeral. I could have been at my own funeral and finally had the send-off that I deserved, along with the others that died for nothing.

SEVERAL DAYS LATER

I watched over my body as it was lowered into my newly made grave. I was buried next to my friend, Erica, which was very thoughtful of Kaiser.

'We are gathered here today to finally let the souls of the past rest. Everyone who is being buried here will never be forgotten. This town is under a new rule now, which means people will only die of natural causes. God rest their souls, and may they find peace in death,' Kaiser said as he put a flower on each of our graves.

I continued to watch, and if I still had feelings, I would have been crying right now because it was so sad to see. I never thought I'd be able to see my own funeral. It made me happier knowing that my husband had been watching down on me ever since he died to make sure that I was okay.

'I can feel Kalina's presence right now, she is still here with us. I know she would be proud of me and everyone that carries on in her name,' Kaiser continued as everyone in the village stood around and paid their respects at the funeral. There were so many bodies being buried, it was enough to break anyone's heart. I was glad that Grindon was dead because he was the cause of all our deaths. I always imagined that being a ghost, if it was possible, would be a good way to still be around. But now that I was a ghost, I just kept thinking how horrible it was to not be able to connect emotionally with anyone, seeing as I was an emotional person.

I couldn't touch anyone, and eventually, I would have to leave the after world and not even be a ghost. It was all a lot to take in, but it was something that I had to accept. But I could only leave the after world once I was ready, and I had accepted my death.

I realised that there was one more thing that I had to do before I could be laid to rest forever. I had to visit my sister. Whether she would be afraid to see my spirit or not, there were a few things that I had to say to her that I wanted to say before I was wrongly killed. She helped Grindon kill me and my unborn child, even though she swore to protect me as my older sister. I closed my eyes, and when I opened them, I was standing beside Grindon's bed where my sister was crying over his body.

'I swear I will find who killed you, and I won't rest until they suffer for taking you away from me. This baby will grow up and know you as I did, and I will make sure that your child will love you like I do,'

Josephine told Grindon's body as she held her stomach and cried into a cloth. I hovered behind her and looked over her shoulder. She must have felt something behind her because she slowly turned around to face me.

'Is someone there?' she asked in a scared voice. I continued to stand behind her as she soon realised that someone was definitely there.

'It's Kalina. Did you really think you could have a part in my death and then never be haunted by me?' I asked as I floated, and she finally made out my face and realised who I was. She backed away and screamed slightly. I realised that a ghost would probably scare most people, just not Kaiser, as he wanted to see my ghost. I kept walking up to her as I backed her into the corner.

'You're dead! What are you doing here? I don't believe in ghosts!' she exclaimed like a frightened little girl. I actually felt evil for haunting someone who was afraid of me, but she did deserve it. She was willing to bring Grindon's baby into this world, but she didn't think twice when she helped to murder mine. Maybe it was time that I got revenge on her and stopped forgiving so easily.

'I am dead, but I am here to tell you that you won't get away with what you did to me! You and Grindon killed me and my baby because I was a threat to Grindon's rule! For as long as you live, you won't get rid of me, I can assure you!' I shouted in my ghostly voice. She went pale and dropped her cloth onto the floor. She closed her eyes and began to cry heavily as though sympathy would work with the dead.

'Please! Forgive me! I am sorry for what I did, but I saw no other way, please just leave me alone and don't hurt me!' she screamed, but I could barely understand her through all the tears. I tried to remain strong and eerie to make her fear me.

Although I couldn't feel anger towards her, I wanted to act as though I did. She deserved no sympathy. The advantage of being a ghost was that I could look however I wanted. If I wanted someone to be afraid of me, I could make myself look more menacing just by thinking about it. But if it was Kaiser, I could make myself look just the way he remembered me. I could also do things without feeling any remorse or guilt. I once read that the more a ghost scares the living, the stronger the spirit gets.

That gave me the perfect idea. I wouldn't just leave now that Kaiser was in charge. In the after world, they said I could leave forever when I thought it was the time, which was when I had no reason to linger around the living. But the more I thought about it, the more I realised that I had the perfect reason to stay around. If I went now, my sister would get away with everything. She would give birth to her baby, raise it, have a happy life, and probably fall in love again. She'd forget about me. But I could punish her by sticking around and making her life hell by haunting her and convincing her that she was going mad. It seemed evil to do that to a member of my own family, but what did I have to lose?

'I won't hurt you, sister. I'm not capable of letting my sister be killed like you were. But you do need to suffer. How about I haunt you for the rest of your days?' I asked as she stared at me and hoped that none of this was real, but it was. No matter what she said, she couldn't talk herself out of this one, and Grindon wasn't there to protect her.

'No, please, I get the message. I'll be a better person from now on, I'll— my sister said as I interrupted her, as I knew she would eventually talk me round, and I had made my mind up.

'NO! You will not get out of this! I will be here watching you all the time, and I will come to you when you aren't expecting it. And when that baby of yours is born, I will use it to live again, seeing as I was wrongly killed. Grindon's baby may as well be of some use to the world,' I said, smirking and looking all evil as my sister looked like she was about to die of fear.

'My baby? What? What … do you mean?' she asked as though she had no idea that what I was going to do was even possible.

'As soon as that baby is born, I will possess the child and bring myself back to life. When I grow up, I will kill you, and I will rule after Kaiser over the next generation, and there is nothing you can do about it. Sleep tight, sister,' I said as I began to laugh uncontrollably.

She screamed and feared the possession of her unborn child. But the scariest thing was, I meant every word. My husband would understand why I wanted a second chance to live, and I would be the next generation when Josephine was grey and old. I was the future of Yalford Valley. My plan to live again was genius and I would be reborn, it was always fate's plan.

STORY 3

YOU MUST SURVIVE

Chapter 1

It was just a normal day, until it wasn't. The sunlight beamed viciously through the kitchen blinds, reflecting on the marble counter. I had the window slightly open, letting in some stale morning air. It hit my face like the cold crisp steel of an axe. It caught my attention; I couldn't look away. I couldn't help but shudder when I noticed the paper that hung loosely on the window ledge.

I grabbed the paper and forcefully slammed the window shut. Having the window open suddenly made me feel uneasy and over exposed. Unsafe. Unhinged. Something was watching, waiting. I stared down at the text until I felt my eyes would bleed if I didn't look away. There was something about the text. I felt it ripping into my soul, taking a blood-stained seat in the forefront of my mind. It was all I could focus on.

"Charlene, you have been chosen" I glared at the letters. *How the hell did it have my name on it?* I turned it over, accidently slitting my finger on the bottom corner. There was nothing but an address, no explanation. The blood began to pour down my finger, I helplessly let out a slight gasp. I couldn't help but notice where my bloody fingerprint had stained the paper. The word "chosen" was perfectly shadowed by blood. I had a sense that something was reaching out to me and pulling me into its darkness. A mysterious force was compelling me to follow the trail. I gave into the unexpected impulse, I let curiosity take over my body.

Without a second thought, I hopped onto the next bus that went to the other end of town. It was almost as if I had suddenly lost control over my body, the control had been given to something else. A feeling of deep dread crept into my body and spread miserably into my veins. The urge to visit this place was becoming overwhelming. But still, there was no backing out of this now. I had to know who had chosen me and what for. I tapped my finger nervously on my seat thinking of nothing but my own fate. Then, I arrived.

The whole journey was somewhat of a conscious blur. The place I had been sent to by something far greater than me. *The town's local abandoned train station? How strange!* I walked a few steps further to investigate, listening to the sound of the worn concrete scratching against my boots. There was nothing before me, just an echo of what used to be. Broken tiled walls, a dusty rail track and the absence of light.

But then, there it was. A train, unlike any other train I'd seen before. It was a vintage train with the word "pullman" written across it. *These types of trains weren't in use by the public, how did it get here?* Without having the chance to process a 1930's pullman train appearing, the tough steel doors widened, inviting me inside.

What are you doing? Do not get on a train in an abandoned station! I ignored my thoughts, forcing myself to take each step until it was too late. I was hit by the overwhelming smell of dusty metal and human sweat. Wait, I wasn't alone.

'Another passenger? Great. Welcome aboard the ghost train or whatever the fuck this is,' a strong male voice muttered behind me.

'What is this? Have I been kidnapped or something?' I asked the people before me. From what I could see, there were around a handful of people on the train. But maybe there were more on a different carriage. My heart fluttered with relief when I realised I wasn't being forced to go through this terrifying experience alone. Perhaps we would get some answers soon.

I heard the screech of the train colliding against the metal tracks, we were on the move.

'Don't ask us. We have been racking our brains trying to figure out what the hell this is! I was doing some shopping when I dropped my purse and came here. I had no control over it! It was like something had possessed me,' a frail old lady said, her voice hardly above a whisper. She looked overly nervous, even more so than me.

This cannot be happening. I ran my fingers through my hair, ruffling it up anxiously. Something had to be going on here, something sinister. Before I had the chance to think any further, a light flashed on the train triggering my full attention. It seemed to be some sort of message.

'Hey guys, look,' the man from earlier said, shaking his finger apprehensively at the red text on the screen.

It read:

"All passengers are on board, let's begin. Get ready for the worst ride of your life."

It flashed for a few seconds and disappeared. It resembled disfigured text on a broken computer screen.

'Well, that's some freaky shit. Who do y'all think is controlling this thing?' The same man called out.

'I don't know but we are in this thing together. We should start with our names, right? I mean that's the polite thing to do. I'm Mary and I'm 72. Anyone else wanna introduce themselves?' Mary suggested politely.

'Whatever, if y'all think it will help. The name's Jonas, I'm a 28-year-old cab driver. Who else we got in here?' Jonas replied, his glare suddenly focused on me.

'I'm... well, I'm Charlene. I'm 30 this year. And I have no idea where I am or what's going on.' I blurted out, sharing more than I intended to.

'None of us do darlin'. We still tryna' figure this shit out. Anyone else got anything to say before this creepy ass train gets even creepier?' Jonas said, his sassy look and confidence radiating in my direction. But nothing could make me feel safe, not even a confident stranger.

'I'm Stephen and I'm freaking the hell out right now. This feels like one of those twisted horror movies,' a timid voice crept up.

I smiled at everyone awkwardly and took another look around, realising that I hadn't bothered to get my bearings. I noticed the posters were peeling from the walls, but they didn't seem as old as the train. *Wait, did pullman trains even have posters?* I knew they were for first class passengers decades ago, but I didn't get how one ended up in this station. *How was it still running? And where the hell was the final stop?* I noticed the blue velvet cushioned seats and the varnished sepia wooden walls. The wooden panelling was beginning to show its age as some of it was oxidised along the bottom. *This was definitely luxurious.*

How someone got hold of a train like this was a mystery to me. It was the sort of thing that would be a part of an exhibit in museums. They continued to introduce themselves, but their voices became just a fragment of noise in my mind. Something else was taking up my head space. An eerie feeling washed over me like a rush of terrifying adrenalin, preparing me for the worst. I looked up at one of the peeling posters, it was an old movie advertisement from the 1930's.

It had the tagline "sometimes, even our pockets hold secrets". The words rung in my mind like blood splattered church bells. Your pockets. I walked to a quiet corner of the train, where nobody's eyes were on me. I unzipped my pocket in my new leather jacket and felt something in there. I've never worn this before so how could something be in the pocket? It felt like a scrunched-up piece of paper, so I pulled it out to look. It was a piece of paper that wasn't there before, but how?

It had perfectly written typewriter text on it, I held it closer to my eyes to ensure I was reading it correctly. "No matter what happens, you must survive. At all costs." I read it over and over in my mind, but the words wouldn't process. *I must survive what?* The dim lights went out, it went pitch black. I had no choice but to welcome the darkness.

Chapter 2

I closed my eyes for a few seconds, but it was not my imagination. This was really happening. The darkness would not fade.

'Who turned the lights out! I can't see a thing!' An unfamiliar voice screeched in the blackness of the unknown.

Although I was surrounded by the cries of those around me, I could hear nothing but my own breathing. Each breath was worryingly shallower than the last. My chest continuously tensed up with every rapid heartbeat. It was beating so fast that I didn't know if it would stop before I figured out what was happening. Then it was over. I expected a sense of relief but all I felt was my body trying to recover. The lights above us flickered on and off, before finally stabilising and lighting up the whole carriage. I finally let out a deep sigh of relief. Nothing could have made this situation any worse except trying to figure it out in the dark.

'Anybody know why the hell the lights went out?' Jonas asked everyone.

'This train is clearly too old and hardly functioning, maybe it's that,' I stated, not managing to keep my words locked inside my mouth as I wanted to.

Before anyone could answer me, the screen flashed. Red warped letters stretched across the screen with the words "sacrifice one" and a timer began. It was a countdown of five minutes. The sight of a timer got me thinking about what I had left behind. I had no idea what time it was and how late I would be for work. My boss was like a second mother to me, and she would panic if I was late, she knew how punctual I was. What about my family? No, I had to get out of here for them. I had to at least try. My thoughts were projected back onto the present moment when I heard Stephen speak.

'Sacrifice one? What the hell! What does it mean?' Stephen asked but the hope drained from his face when he realised that nobody else had any answers either.

5 minutes to sacrifice what? Surely not a human being? Maybe the paper from my pocket and the timer are...connected?

'We really need to figure this shit out, yeah? Because this train is travelling at like a really fast speed and it's making me uneasy. The windows are blacked out and now there's some creepy timer counting down. I need to get home for my wife's hospital appointment, so let's find a way out of here!' Jonas said as I noticed some sweat droplets were beginning to frame his face.

I doubt anyone else had a random piece of paper in their pocket demanding that they had to survive. I need to hide it. I screwed the piece of paper up and stuffed it into my back pocket, hoping I was too fast for anyone to notice. But my hopes were crushed when I heard the subtle sound of it hitting the floor behind me. I clearly didn't put the paper in deep enough. What would that little mistake cost me?

'Paper? What does it say? Where did you find it?' Mary asked relentlessly.

She dashed over to me and retrieved the crumpled paper from the worn carpet that covered the length of the train. I watched her face sink to panic as she read the words.

'What is this? Are you in on this whole thing or something? What exactly do we need to survive!' Mary yelled, her voice resembling a yelp. Something about the way she spoke didn't feel sincere to me, but I couldn't accuse a stranger of lying based on nothing but my instincts. I was in enough trouble.

'No, wait. I am just as confused as you are about this. I found it in my pocket just now. Maybe it's a clue? The movie poster was a clue so maybe we should look at the other posters to see if they mean anything.'

My voice trembled as I tried to speak, they had to know I was innocent, and I wanted this to be over just as much as them.

2 minutes left. But what happens at zero?! Maybe it's a hoax? Mary passed the paper to Jonas and then to the others that had barely muttered a word since I arrived.

'Is that what this is? Some sort of wicked joke! This better be a joke lady, or you will be in some serious shit! You can't just kidnap people like this and try to kill us and—' Jonas yelled in my face, hardly taking a breath.

'Just stop! I have no idea what's going on here! All I know is that the writing on that poster up there led me to check my pocket. Like some sort of instinct. Then I found the paper. I don't know what it means, and I certainly didn't plan this whole thing! I'm just a normal woman who works in a clothes store. I'm not the enemy here,' I pleaded. I felt as though a tear would form in my eye if I continued, so I stopped talking to gain composure.

'Everyone, check your pockets now! I need to know if this woman is full of shit!' Jonas' voice echoed across the train.

They checked and checked again. Nothing. Damn it. Why was it just me that got a note like that?

'See? Nobody else has anything, just you. Surely you realise how suspicious that looks? The countdown is at one minute, what happens when the timer runs out? You better start talking, lady,' Jonas said, edging closer to me and making me feel his intended intimidation.

'I honestly don't know anything. All I know is I'm in the same position as the rest of you. I don't know what the countdown is for or what will happen next. I'm terrified, just like all of you,' I told them honestly, backing away towards the back of the train like a frightened animal.

'We only have 20 seconds left! It said sacrifice one, so we need to choose one person and quick!' Stephen called out, the name badge on his pearly white shirt shimmering under the train lights.

I let my eyes search up and down the train for answers, but nothing stood out. There was no time to check the posters for more clues but maybe they were right, maybe the posters were just random. *Maybe the poster mentioning pockets was just a coincidence after all. I stared at the timer as I watched it count down miserably for the last 5 seconds. Maybe nothing would happen? Maybe we were fine, and this was all some sick joke.* I noticed Jonas staring right past me towards the wall.

'Wait. There's a line on the floor and it says sacrifice on the wall. We can't trust her, let's use her as a test, see what happens? We are already out of options, what choice do we have?' Jonas suggested.

'That's sick! She's a human being, no matter how suspicious she may be. Let's think this through,' Stephen counteracted, his voice young and croaky but he seemed to be the only person fighting in my corner.

'There's no time. We have 5 seconds!' Jonas yelled, panic possessing his eyes wildly.

I looked over at Mary hoping she would be the voice of reason. A kind, frail old lady would surely be against murder which was where this seemed to be heading. Not a murmur came out of her mouth, she just backed off behind Jonas and pressed her back against the wall. I tried to back away to escape the danger but there was nowhere else to go. I felt his hand forcefully shoving me backwards, causing me to bang my spine against a pole. Not one of the other passengers tried to make him see reason. I fell to the floor and felt nothing but shock and pain. Why do they think I'm the enemy here? I glanced at the clock as it counted the final second.

I closed my eyes as the timer beeped twice, making my ear drums feel as though they would burst at any moment. But then, bang! A split second of agony rushed through my body intensely. So intense that I felt as though my skull had been ripped apart and my brain had been mutilated. The pain was unbearable and like no other. I registered the horrified faces that stood before me until my eyes forced themselves shut. Then, nothing. I was no more. It was over.

Chapter 3

2 YEARS AGO

I put the clothes back onto the rack and stared into the distance. How many more customers would I have to serve before I could leave? I sighed and walked back up to the till.

'Aren't you a pretty young thing?' A little old lady said to me as she passed me a thrilly skirt to scan. I smiled gracefully.

'Thank you,' I replied. She handed me the worn money and I gave her the receipt.

'You are destined for great things my darling, keep following the right path and one day, you will be a hero. Just remember to always make good moral decisions,' The woman said, her smile stretching to her ears but strangely, not her eyes. The smile almost looked forced.

'I'm sorry? I'm nothing special, I'm just a woman trying to get by,' I explained politely.

She shook her head with sincere disapproval.

'You must believe you are special, if you don't, the whole world could suffer. And remember, not everything in life is literal sometimes, it's just a test.'

She gave me a cautious wink. She grabbed her skirt and rushed out of the store.

Just a test? A hero? What on Earth did she mean by that?

NOW

My eyes flung open aggressively as though barbed wire was forcefully prising my eyelids open. The pain, the unbearable wretched pain had disappeared. Here I was. *How was I still...breathing?* I stretched my hands out in front of me and wiggled my fingers a few times. I glared down at my chest and double checked that my lungs were still taking in oxygen. Maybe I wasn't breathing, maybe I had lost my mind.

Maybe I didn't die at all. But here I was standing outside the same train that I had just died in. *That's if I did die. Surely not or why would I be here? Maybe it was all just a bad dream?* I sniggered to myself and nervously shook off the idea that I was back from the dead. I also ignored the strange feeling of DeJa'Vu, and my feet carried me onto the train once again, against my own free will. I had completely lost control of myself.

'Another passenger? Great. Welcome aboard the ghost train or whatever the fuck this is,' a confident voice said.

His voice felt familiar to me, a sound that grated heavily on every fibre of my being. Everything about this scene felt all too familiar. My instincts led me to feel around in my pocket. There was the paper. I shoved it back down into my pocket, hoping it would somehow get lost in the seam. What was happening here? Why did this all feel familiar as though I had lived it before? My gaze locked to the end of the train, the line. Something ghastly happened here, I could feel it. No way. A vision of a bullet being fired into the back of my skull filled my mind like fresh dirt piling onto a coffin. I died, I definitely died. I remembered feeling my body shut down in that final moment. So how was I still living? None of this made sense.

'Do you have anything to say? Or are you planning on staring out of the window all day? We are trying to figure out what is going on here! All we know is that this train is vintage, a classy one for first class passengers only. We can't seem to figure anything else out,' a woman yelled. I looked up and remembered her, her name was Mary, the one who didn't seem to care if I lived or died.

'I know this might sound strange, but have we met before?' I asked, scrunching my face up with pure confusion and dread.

'No? None of us on this train have met before. We just got led here, we don't know how or why. But the doors are locked, there's no way out. It only opens to let people in, then it shuts tight again,' Stephen explained.

I felt my bones tremble beneath my enervated skin. My eyes flashed around the train in search of much needed answers. The same question crossed my mind over and over; how? How was I back here after dying? How was any of this possible? How did they not recognise me? I would drown in the questions as I assumed nobody on the train would have any answers. I forced myself to take a much-needed deep breath, not realising the racing thoughts in my mind sent me into a panicking frenzy. I felt fate's firm hand wrap around my throat and squeeze the life out of me. I needed to get my bearings in case it happened again.

I began to pace up and down the train, absorbing the faces of those that were facing this nightmare with me. I needed to look long and hard to find anything that was distinctive about the train. Even finding out the destination would be a revelation.

'Anyone got any clue about where this thing is taking us?' I asked everyone calmly.

'We are clueless, just like you. I hardly even remember getting on this train. We were trying to come up with a plan, but we haven't got very far,' Stephen answered nervously.

Why was everyone else on the train so quiet? There were only three people that had spoken, that had to be significant somehow. My attention was stolen by an urge to look at the window to my left side. A puff of condensation had created some letters, I stared closely to focus my vision. It read: "keep quiet to live". *Keep quiet to live? Who was telling me these things? Was someone on this train messing with me?* I finally tore myself away from the smeared writing on the window and turned back to face everyone.

'Can anyone else see that? Who could have left that message?' I asked, pointing to the window beside me.

Mary gave me a look of distrust before taking several steps forward to the window that I was pointing at. She stared over at me with a blank expression.

'Now is hardly the time to be playing games! Stop wasting our time!' Mary said, she walked in the opposite direction.

When I looked at the window again, it was clear. No writing, no condensation, no sign that I was telling the truth. Was I losing my mind? My muscles tensed, causing my whole body to lock ferociously into place. My body had completely disconnected from my brain's commands, causing me to be incapable of going after Mary to explain what I saw.

It was as though something was pulling my feet forwards, step by step, forcing me to go further into the unknown. I heard distorted voices in the background talking about the timer, it had begun. But all I could concentrate on was getting to my new destination on the train, wherever that was.

My legs came to a halt eventually, right at the other end of the train. I found my hand reaching down to a seat to my right. I pulled out a map that sat neatly underneath and I suddenly felt my self-control flood back to me like a gush of violent midnight breeze. I had no idea how I was finding these things, but I had a feeling it was completely impossible. I swiftly unravelled the map, trying to see through the creases and small rips.

The only thing that stood out to me was a big black cross with the words "the end of the line" scribbled next to it. It sat perfectly in the middle of the map but nothing else caught my attention. By the way the map was designed, only one thing was crystal clear; we were on a loop; there was no destination. So, what was the point in being on a train?

Nobody to rescue us, nobody to hear our screams. We were completely alone. We were lost with little hope. My intense grip of the map loosened, and I heard it gently tap against the floor as untold memories came flooding back to me like a burst riverbank. *Jonas. I remembered! He was the reason I died! He was a danger to me!* How could I be so sure that he wouldn't sacrifice me again? I glanced over at the timer, only 25 seconds left. I had been in my own world for almost 4 minutes!

I had to think, and I had to think fast! The first time this happened, something made me walk here and get on this train. I dropped the note and they noticed it, making them not trust me. Jonas turned aggressive and sacrificed me without a second thought. But they still had something against me, I could feel it. I didn't want to hurt anyone, but I couldn't take the risk. If I was killed again, I would be back to square one. No answers, no way of finding out what happened after the timer, nothing.

I looked over and saw Mary and Jonas whispering and still, nobody else seemed to have anything to say. My eyes locked onto the timer, unable to blink or revert them away. 10 seconds left. It was now or never. It didn't feel right but nothing about this did. It was him or me. A deep exhale escaped my lungs and I charged towards him, trying not to think of what sort of a person this would turn me into.

Mary stepped aside as I almost took Jonas off his feet. The strength I suddenly showed was a shock to me, but I had no time to stop and think. I plunged towards him; I couldn't help but take in his facial expression; afraid, terrified, haunted. How could I do this to another human being? *No. He did this to me first. I had to do this for me, to survive. He had already shown that he was a direct threat to my survival, one of us had to die.*

I dismissed the look on his face and any rational thinking. When I focused again and finally stood still for a moment, it was done. I had charged into him, sweeping him off his feet and throwing him over the sacrifice line. He was a pig, forced into the slaughterhouse. I heard a gasp from Mary as she covered her mouth and turned away.

I wanted to look away, but I couldn't. My sight was transfixed on watching him die, the way I had died. The sound of the bullet sent a shuddering shock wave through my body, making my muscles turn to jelly and my brain almost switch off with disgust. I watched him grow desperate and helpless, pitiful even. His eyes closed and his lifeless body slumped to the ground with a thud. I watched the blood pour out from the back of his skull as it stained everything, including my mind.

'You evil little… You are a killer! Why did you do that?' Mary yelled in my face. I concentrated on her words but none of them sunk in.

Maybe she was right, maybe I was a killer now. I heard a noise which resembled the creakiness of an old door opening. I looked at the sacrifice line and a latch opened, Jonas' body fell through it and then it slammed shut. *We were being killed, a bullet to the back of the head. Then our bodies were just thrown on a track in the middle of nowhere. No humanity or anything, just prepared for the next victim.*

'You don't understand. You could never understand what I just went through. I didn't want to kill him, but I had to. I had to see what would happen next!' I shouted towards her. My emotions caused me to drown in my own words. Then, it started again. No break in between, just the same clock counting down until the next person's time was up. Stephen had turned into a blubbering mess. His long-sleeved shirt had turned into a tissue for his damp nose and his bottom lip couldn't stop quivering. This would scar him for life, just like the rest of us. That decision wasn't easy, but I had to do it.

'How did you even know to throw him over that line to kill him? Huh? Are you behind this whole thing?' Mary asked.

Her suspicions were fair, but I had no intention of reassuring her. Why should I? She would likely sacrifice me next anyway. Plus, it seemed that I wasn't here to make friends, just to survive and get myself out of this mess.

'It's complicated, okay? You wouldn't even believe me.' I replied, choosing to say as little as possible in response.

The train fell silent, we both stared at the clock as though it would decide who was next for us.

'I refuse to choose, I won't. Let's just see what happens when the timer runs out. It can't kill us if we haven't crossed the line, right?' Stephen suggested, his body not giving him a break to breathe in between uncontrollable shaking. He hadn't taken his eyes off the marked blood on the carpet since Jonas was killed. This experience was already beginning to haunt him.

Maybe he was right, every theory deserved to be tested. So, we waited. Every second felt like an hour. The seconds painfully ticked away, and we had no choice but to watch. It finally reached zero and then nothing. A delightful smile crossed my lips and a sigh escaped from my dry mouth. We did it, we had won. All we had to do was choose not to sacrifice anyone! Jonas didn't have to die, but I couldn't think about that right now. My moment of glory was cut short when a red light blinded us and began to flicker around the train, darting back and forth between the people that had not yet spoken. *What was this? Was it over or was there more?* Nothing was happening, we had won! All we had to do was let the timer run out!

All of a sudden, everyone turned around at once as though they were in perfect synchronisation. Then it dawned on me. *They hadn't moved yet or spoken or anything because something was stopping them.* They finally took very slow steps towards us, but their mouths were taped shut and their hands were behind their backs. The three of us took a cautious step back, Stephen cowered behind me like a wounded schoolboy. I wondered what could possibly be worse than what we had just been through. The red light flashed all over the place until it finally stopped in the middle of the people. We then heard a robotic voice coming from the timer screen. *Was someone watching us this whole time?*

'Well done. You worked it out. But it won't always be that easy. Now, get ready for stage two,' the robotic voice stated, making me forget a human was responsible for all this.

I stared over at Mary; my mouth slightly open as I tried to take in the fact that this was far from over. Why did they have the rest of the passengers tied up and gagged when we were free to move and speak? How did the passengers know when to act? Did it mean they were in on this? I needed answers, I craved them. But right now, the only thing that mattered was surviving stage two and figuring out why I was alive after dying. I had to survive this or so the universe told me.

Chapter 4

6 YEARS AGO

'Do you have a train ticket madam?' The train conductor asked me.

I rummaged through my handbag and tried to find it, but it was nowhere to be seen. Where could it have gone? I was too busy worrying about stepping on a train. Knowing my friend was already on it made it a little more comforting.

'I'm terribly sorry, I seem to have lost it somehow,' I replied, panic burning in my chest.

'Okay well then I am afraid you will have to buy another ticket. What is your destination?' He said, tapping the electronic device as he spoke. He grabbed onto the rail near me to keep his balance.

'The end of the line. I'm getting off at the last stop,' I said. I noticed a slight twitch in his eye as he digested my words.

'The end of the line? You know what they say about that. She that reaches the end of the line is granted a new lease of life. I'd hold onto that if I were you, you may need the reminder one day,' He told me. I tapped my card on the screen and paid for yet another ticket.

'I've never heard of that one, but if you say so,' I said with slight laughter creeping into my voice.

As he walked away, I looked up at the poster as I walked closer to my seat where my friend was sitting. I stared at the words until they engraved themselves into my mind. It read: "stay alive for them" and a woman was embracing her family. I guess it was strange what we lived for.

NOW

The unanswered questions burned through my brain like a deadly bolt of lightning. I had to know why I was here and what it all meant but I knew nobody would tell me, at least not yet.

'Stage two? I thought it was over! Why are they tied up?' Stephen bellowed, his voice vibrating against the outer shell of the train.

The same robotic voice began to speak, and the words flashed on the screen again. It read: "it's you or them". I let the words swirl around in my mind for a few seconds like a deadly cocktail before they were swallowed in one vicious gulp. Either us or the hostages had to die, that was the only way to win this round.

'Did you see what it said? It's us or them, how do we decide something like that?' I asked, I allowed the emotion to leak from my shaky voice.

'Wait, look! The sacrifice line has disappeared! What the…there are red lines forming in the middle of the train!' Mary yelled.

I followed her finger to see where she was pointing. Thin red lines were beginning to separate us from the hostages. Lasers. We either found a way to survive or we would be chopped into pieces by a laser.

'Nobody go near them; I think they are lasers. We really need to think about this!' I replied.

I glanced up at the clock and it began to count down from 10 minutes. 10 minutes is all we had to decide if our lives were worth more than somebody else's. Would this be it? Or would I miraculously come back to life again? I still felt the fear of death creating a tornado of dread inside me, it was too much of a risk to take. Maybe I didn't die from the bullet, maybe that was a dream, and this was reality. We had no time to think, only act! Was this round supposed to put us up against each other or was there a way to work together and all survive? The ties around their wrists suddenly snapped off, they could move. They no longer looked so vulnerable.

'Okay, okay. Let's just think for a second. They are no longer in immediate danger now, right? So we don't need to go over there and rescue them. We could just wait around and see what happens when the timer runs out,' Mary suggested.

'No, we can't. Whoever is doing this to us went to great lengths to somehow get lasers onto a moving train, they aren't here for show. The only way for someone to survive this round is to make the lasers disappear before the timer runs out,' I explained.

'Maybe Mary is right. Why should we risk our lives for strangers? Maybe they're in on it. Who knows?' Stephen interjected.

As he finished speaking, he aggressively slapped my shoulder and forced me to turn around.

'Look! There's a new green line that has replaced the sacrifice line and it says survivors! Whoever passes that line survives the round! What are we waiting for? Let's just walk over there now!' Stephen yelled, he began to tug at my clothes and edge me towards the end of the train.

'What? No. There will be consequences, there always is. There's no way it would be that easy. Plus, I can't live with myself knowing I'd just left people to die like that,' I counteracted. Mary kept her mouth shut all of a sudden as she focused more on the ground than our conversation.

'They'll be fine if they don't go near the lasers! Come on, it's probably just a test to see what we do again. We need to choose ourselves here! Please! I'm so young, I can't die on this train, I won't!' Stephen said as panic began to override his face.

'Stop this! I couldn't live with that! Think about it! Why would they place some hostages on this train just for us to walk in the opposite direction and only save ourselves? I get that you are scared but we need to think about this. Their lives are just as important as ours! The last round was some sort of mind game, maybe this one is the same.' I explained, hoping to see compassion forming in his eyes instead of just raw fear. There was nothing. It felt as though I was staring into a black hole. Maybe his mind was already made up.

'Okay, fine, I hear you. You can't blame me for thinking of myself and being terrified of the possibility of dying brutally on this train. But they better cross the lasers and quickly. They only have 7 and a half minutes. You better be right on this,' Stephen finally agreed.

I let myself drop to my knees as I crawled gently towards the lasers to study them. I glanced up at Mary and noticed her continuous silence. I had obviously never seen real life lasers before and I didn't know what staring at them would do, but something was urging me to look closer. Something was telling me that this wasn't as simple as it looked.

'I know this is difficult but could one of you edge a little closer to the lasers please, I need to be sure of something first,' I commanded.

All four of them shuffled a little closer, one of their heads almost touched the first laser. A loud zapping sound erupted from the lasers, and they all flashed, turned blood red and looked as though they were burning. I stared at the steam that radiated off them.

'Wait! Get back, get back!' I yelled; I couldn't stand the thought of my command putting them in further danger.

As they backed off from the lasers, they returned to a light orange colour with no more heat around them. I took a deep breath and gently waved my hand in the air, edging closer to the laser nearest to me.

'What are you doing! You could get yourself killed!' I heard Stephen's voice bellow behind me.

'I just have a feeling about something, just wait and I'll—' I said with my eyes closed as I felt the heat of the laser against my finger.

As I got a little too close to the lasers, they began to light up green and they looked less dangerous. I smiled as my theory was proven to be correct.

'Traffic light lasers, clever,' I said as I jumped up from my knees, suddenly feeling confident that I could save the hostages.

'What? You aren't making sense! How do you figure things out so fast? Wait, traffic light lasers? So, if they turn green, it's fine to move?' Stephen questioned, his innocent baby face suddenly booming with hope.

'I'm not really sure about that part but I guess it's trial and error. From what I can gather, we can only turn off the lasers from our side. If nobody is near them, they remain orange. If the hostages get closer, they turn red and deadly. If we go near them, they go green meaning they are safe. Kind of,' I stated confidently.

Stephen closed his eyes, rubbed his forehead and stuttered before forcing his words out.

'We only have 7 minutes left, it took us a good three minutes to work it out, well, for you to work it out. Doesn't it seem a little too simple though? That all we have to do is kneel down near a laser and the hostages can just crawl through and join us?' Stephen said.

I shook my head and wished that things could always be that easy.

'Unfortunately not, that would be too easy. There has to be some sort of risk involved. But not something overly complicated or they would give us longer than 10 minutes,' I replied as I stared around the train hoping for another hint as to what to do next. I took another look at Mary and wondered why she was so quiet all of a sudden. *Why wasn't she contributing to anything we said?*

'Mary? Do you have anything to say? We all need to agree on what to do,' I asked.

She didn't answer. She sighed heavily and shook her head, not even bothering to make eye contact with me. Why had she gone so quiet all of a sudden?

Time was running out and so were my theories. With no wisdom from Mary, it was down to Stephen and I. My head automatically turned to my right-hand side, where my vision locked onto a tiny hole in the train with a bright orange light coming from it. Strange. It almost looked like a projection. Then it hit me. It seemed too much of a coincidence for there to be a random orange coloured projection coming from a hole and have the same colour lasers. Perhaps the lasers weren't real and there was no real danger after all? I got back down to my hands and knees and began to slowly place my little finger on one of the lasers.

'Now what are you doing! This is no time for playing around, we need to decide what we are doing! You'll get yourself killed!' Stephen called out.

I was too busy sorting through my thoughts to let his words take over my mind. I squinted and prepared myself to feel the intense pain of my finger being torn in half, but nothing happened. No pain, no disfigured finger and no heat. It was a fake laser. I smiled and wafted the same finger onto the next laser, but I jumped back in agony. I held my finger tightly as blood began to pour. A slit was made down my finger but luckily, it was still attached to my hand. If one laser did nothing and another laser cut me, it could only mean one thing. We had to take risks and work out which lasers were projections, and which weren't. Only then could we get safely across to collect the hostages and bring them to the survivor's line. This was tough, very tough. It had turned into a choice between us and them.

'I knew it would be more complicated than we thought! Some lasers are just projections and others are real. We would have to risk our lives or serious injury to get them all across safely,' I said in a worried tone.

'Exactly! Come on! We don't have time for a big moral discussion here. Let's just get over the line and leave them. Who knows? Maybe they will survive after all. Maybe if they stay at that side and let the time run out, they will make it, but we have to go now!' Stephen yelled. The pressure of his voice rang in my ears and left a heavy mark on my conscience.

He began to pace towards the survivor's line. I could tell he wasn't a bad guy, but the pressure of the situation had completely taken over his moral compass. I doubt he would have been able to live with himself if he went through with this. I looked over at the hostages who were standing hopelessly, holding their hands out to us, their eyes begging us not to leave them.

Who would I become if I just left them there like that? I stopped and realised that I had already begun to follow him because I knew it was the best chance of survival. Any human would consider the easy option in these circumstances. I was ashamed of my body for forcing me to pick myself over everyone else. I was better than that.

Once I realised what I was doing, I stopped and spun around to face them. Their desperate eyes were filled with need. Who were we to decide who lived and who died? They wanted to live just as much as us and they had every right to. I paced back over to the lasers and fell back to my knees. Mary slowly crossed the survivor's line, without uttering a single word.

'No, we all need to agree on this and stick together! You're making the wrong decision here!' Stephen's voice echoed on the train of secrets.

'He's right, they aren't worth your life. Come on, let's hurry up and get this round over with,' Mary finally said.

I chose to let their words drown into nothingness; I wouldn't allow them to reach my ears.

Which one was a projection? How could I save them without harming myself in the process? I had to do this. I had to take a leap of faith and go with my instincts. Where were the signs from the universe when you needed them? I half expected something on the train to advise me on what to do but nothing arrived. I didn't have the time to wait, the timer was ticking down quickly.

'I know it's scary for you all to trust a stranger with your lives but I'm all you have. Please, trust me enough to get you all across that line. Take a leap of faith with me,' I told them with a warm welcoming smile spreading across my face.

I took a deep breath and faced the lasers so that my face was almost touching it. I could hear Stephen cursing me in the background, but his words no longer mattered to me. I closed my eyes and crawled forward. The laser lights turned red unexpectedly. I felt a gory heat rush through me. But how? Activating them from this side made them green and safe to cross! I gasped, knowing what would come next. It was the end.

I heard frail squeals of fear coming from the passengers. I couldn't breathe, speak or move. Was this it? I had no choice but to listen to Mary's words, they suffocated the silence and took over.

'You should have come with us over this safe survivor's line. Did you know the laser controls are over here? Hmm. Didn't think so. More fool you. I'd say see you around but guess not,' Mary's voice haunted my mind as I entered extreme distress.

The pain was unthinkable yet quick. I felt my limbs be dismembered from my body. The sound resembled animal guts squelching and dropping to the floor. A soft, mushy gory sound. It reminded me that I was nothing but skin, bone and guts and I was fragile. My eyes remained open as death creeped up on me. The sound of my own violent death would be the last thing I ever heard.

Chapter 5

3 DAYS AGO

Everything was ready. I had always had a deep fear of trains but if my best friend wanted me to visit her, I would. I had a habit of letting my fears get the better of me, but not this time. I was done with enjoying the odd phone call once a week with her, it was time to see Lindsey in person. It was only an hour away on the train, surely, I could survive for that long. I dragged myself to my local train station, a sight I had not seen for 6 years since I last faced my fears and stepped onto a train. I ended up having a panic attack and getting off early. I opened up to Lindsey once and said I was terrified of trains, but she just laughed, I could never understand insensitive people. What was it about them? People always asked me. The only answer I could come up with was having no control. No control over speed, how crowded they got or anything. I left out the part about how just looking at the front end of them scared me, a very intimidating vehicle.

I sat in the train station staring down at my silver-plated watch. I watched it tick away the seconds. The train was due in less than five minutes, the sooner the better. The only thing worse than facing your fears was waiting too long to face them. Lindsey would text me soon to reassure me that everything would be okay. I began to nervously bounce my leg as people paced past me, looking as though they had too much on their minds to even stop to think. A crushing feeling of immense dread began to drain my energy, like a vampire's victim having the last droplet of blood drawn from their dry veins. I was running out of time. Nothing in the world could have saved me now. I was savagely clawed back from my thoughts when my phone pinged. *Was it Lindsey?* Unfortunately, it wasn't, it was just an alert for a news article. The heading was, "Five more people vanish without a trace." I was too curious not to click on it and find out more.

"Concern grows as a total of 12 people have now gone missing from Southern England in just a week. Families have gathered today to give a speech to the nation to find out where their loved ones may be. Leah Sands, a 31-year-old woman has spoken on social media about her older sister, Amelia Sands who is among the missing persons.

She wrote: 'To all that know Amelia, she is a kind and sensible lady, and she would never go off alone for this long. Today marks the 5th day of her disappearance and there are no signs of where she could have gone. My mother says she was acting strange when visiting her, just 12 hours before she disappeared. She kept saying she was getting signs from beyond and had impulses she couldn't control. We assume poor Amelia has suffered from a breakdown and may be in a vulnerable state. If you see her, please take her to the nearest hospital and contact us. Thank you.'

My reading time was sliced in half when the train came to a halt as it screeched against the tracks. The vibrating sound of the metal resembled the final deadly ring of a church bell. The time had come. *Come on, it's not that hard. Just a few steps and you'll be on the train. Don't even think about it.* I found myself steadily rising from the seat that I believed I would cling to. I watched as crowds charged past me and went through the doors. Was I making this into something it wasn't? I drew a few deep breaths each time I forced one foot forward. I was finally there, right by the doors. I was about to do it! They all said I would never get over this fear, but I was about to prove them wrong!

'I wouldn't if I were you,' a crisp and raw voice echoed in my ear.

I jumped back slightly, becoming completely distracted from the task at hand. I turned around to put a face to the sinister voice. It was a slender dark-haired man with a grey tint to his skin. There was a certain professionalism about him that captured my attention and held it hostage. My eyes wouldn't dare look away for fear of dangerous consequences.

'Sorry?' I asked with narrowed brows.

'They are dangerous things. Don't you think? There's just something about them. A mystery of time,' he told me.

'I suppose there is, yes. I am trying to overcome my fear of them. I've been wanting to see my friend for a while now, but she moved away so now, I have to catch a train to see her,' I openly replied to him. *Why did I always open up to strangers?*

'That is a shame, I must say. I try to avoid travelling on trains, they are just too dangerous and not many people understand that. Unless they are forced onto one from something other than their own choice,' he looked away as he spoke in a dramatic way.

'You try to avoid travelling on them and yet here you are on a train platform? What gives there?' I curiously asked.

'I am a mystery and that is how I prefer to stay. Shame about the missing folks though, isn't it?' He told me with a spine-chilling smirk suffocating his face.

'I heard about them; they've been all over the news. It is definitely a shame. I hope they are found soon,' I agreed.

'I heard they were all last seen at this very station, such a coincidence, isn't it?' He muttered.

'How do you know that? The news said nobody knows where they were last seen?' I asked, my voice began to shake as I wondered how he got such information.

He aggressively patted the side of his nose to let me know that it was somehow a big secret and none of my business. He then began to walk in the opposite direction. *Why would he come over here just to have a conversation with me about trains? What was his agenda?* I looked up and realised that the train was leaving. I had missed my chance yet again. No matter what I did, something always stopped me from getting on a train. Why? I did always believe in fate, maybe I was never meant to get on that train. I sighed and slumped myself back down onto a platform seat and ragged my phone out from the deep depths of my pockets.

I went onto Lindsey's messages and warned her that I wouldn't be coming over today after all. I was tired of the constant disappointments that I caused others. I was tired of being afraid of nothing. I had been overly paranoid about everything for a few months now but no matter how many times I warned people that there was doom on the horizon for me, they cast my opinion aside. They refused to believe that I could sense these things, but the awful truth was that I could. No matter what anyone told me, I could feel it getting closer by the day. It wouldn't be long now until I was proven right and that was the day, I dreaded the most.

Chapter 6

A deep breath of dread shot through me like a bullet leaving a pulsating wound. I was reborn. My eyes opened and enlarged to scan the area. Mary was standing next to me, staring over at the hostages. I attempted to hide how breathless I felt to avoid suspicion.

'Stage two? I thought it was over! Why are they tied up?' Stephen bellowed; his speech felt all too familiar.

Everything felt exactly the same. But then I remembered. *Somehow, Mary knew how to get past this round, and she was happy to kill me. I died because of her! I had to find out who she really was. Was Stephen fine with her killing me?*

The flashing of the screen saying "it's you or them" distracted me from my dark thoughts. I knew how this round would play out if Mary had her way again, I had to do something. What did she have against me? If the button was near the survivor's line, why didn't she save us all? With one flick of that switch, all of us could have been saved but she deliberately chose to be the lone survivor. *Why? Was this all about sick mind games?*

'It's okay Mary. Let's not give them the satisfaction. We've got this,' I confidently stated.

A look of confusion washed over her. Stephen looked at me, the fear draining from his face as though I was suddenly his hero. For once, I had the upper hand. Neither of them had any idea what I was up to.

'What do you mean? There is a timer up there! How are you so confident that we can survive this round just like the last one?' She asked me.

'Yeah, are you saying you have a solution for this round and none of us are in danger?' Stephen asked me timidly.

I thought carefully before I attempted to answer. Anything I said could have been used against me if I wasn't careful. *There had to be a reason why she knew about the switch, and I didn't.*

'Forget about the timer and the lasers. We don't need to worry about any of that because we are going to save everyone right this second,' I demanded. My tone was borderline aggressive; I let it harshly levitate towards their ears.

A look of intense stress crashed into Mary's face like the force of a tidal wave. I could almost see her questions darting back and forth in her mind. The question was, what would she ask me first? Or would she carry on pretending that she knew nothing?

'You are not making any sense. There are lasers over there and some hostages. We need to figure out what we are doing and fast! Do we even need to save them?' She asked. But this time, I knew they could be saved.

I sighed and bolted over to the other side of the train where the survivors' line reflected in my eyes. I smiled with intense relief as I noticed the switch that she arrogantly told me about just before I died. I was completely reassured to know that I had full control this time and there was no need for anyone to die.

I watched her eyes follow me across the train without blinking. Did she know what I was about to do? I stopped when I got to the switch. I hovered my hand over it.

'Hmm strange. Did you know there was a switch near the survivor's line? There's red or green. I guess the aim of this game is to just choose to save everyone,' I planted the words into her mind and allowed them to grow.

Stephen began to look just as confused as I felt. *He had to be innocent in all this.*

'How could I have known a switch was there? There has to be a catch! The game wouldn't be that simple, not again. Let's not use the switch, just in case,' Mary squirmed.

I observed her body language closely. She was gently flapping her arms as she spoke and nervously twitching her top lip. She knew I was onto her. *Did that mean I was in even more danger?*

'Why are you so sure that the switch is too dangerous to use? It seems simple to me. We use the switch, the lasers stay green, and they all cross safely, and we all survive,' I confidently stated.

Mary began to repeatedly shake her head as she took several steps backwards.

'How did you find that switch? This makes no sense,' Mary asked, her voice suddenly frailer.

'Can someone please tell me what is going on here? Can't we just use the switch, rescue the hostages and get over the line before the timer runs out?' Stephen answered.

'We could, that would be the simple option. But I need answers. Mary here has a lot of secrets that she'd rather keep hidden,' I replied smugly.

'You must be the one he's been looking for, that's the only way you'd know about it. The dreams were right,' Mary said, just above a whisper.

It seemed that the more I uncovered, the more questions I had. Who was "he"? What did she think I knew? I had to play my cards very close to my chest or this could turn out even worse than last time. I took a deep breath and tried to think carefully about how to handle this. The hostages would suffer if I got this wrong.

'What? You're not making sense! I spotted this switch, that's all there is to it. Now, do you want to explain who you're talking about?' I asked sensibly.

'You don't understand! If I tell you, I'll die too. It would make him not trust me! I swore I'd see this whole game through efficiently!' She screeched. The cracking in her voice was almost unbearable, it made her words seem almost slurred.

I gently laid my hand upon the switch and looked over at the hostages. They had been listening to our conversation and knew how to win this round. I could see that they were just as terrified as me.

'Give me one good reason why I shouldn't press this switch, get the hostages over the survivors line and make the lasers go red on you instead. I haven't trusted you since I met you and now, I know why. You're hiding something and if you don't tell me what, I won't hesitate to sacrifice you,' I explained. My tone had completely switched from compassionate to threatening.

'Wow, you're both crazy!' Stephen yelled, visibly shaking.

I watched her swallow hard and look back and forth from me to the hostages. She was contemplating whether she could risk not telling me. I noticed her observing me and wondering whether I really was capable of killing her just because of a lack of trust.

'Fine, I'll tell you. But I have to survive this! I will have to report to him once all this is over! If he knows that I told you, he'll kill me too.' She told me. For some reason, I believed every word. The fake demeanour had suddenly disappeared and had been replaced with a sincerity that I hadn't seen in her before. She then continued, 'but if you want to know, Stephen has to be the next to die.'

I guess the real question was could I trust her and was it worth taking another life for?

Chapter 7

3 DAYS AGO

How could I tell anyone about this? What was my excuse? I have an irrational fear of trains and that is why I can't go out and socialise like other people? Not to mention the burning pit of dread in my stomach that wouldn't shift. I turned the key in my front door and headed into my safe space, away from any threats or people that didn't believe me. I almost dived onto the couch as I let the feeling of freedom take over me. The relief I felt when I was no longer faced with that vehicle was astonishing. But I knew nobody would ever understand, how could they? I had sent Lindsey a text on the way home saying my train was cancelled.

She trusted me that much that I doubt she'd ever question my integrity. I turned the television on and tried to wind down after quite a stressful morning. I hoped that the feeling of being a failure would eventually fade. The news channel was already on, so I listened carefully.

'Reports have come in about an abandoned train station where a 1930's pullman train has been seen leaving multiple times in the past few days. The train station, formally known as "Lenton's Cross" has been abandoned since the late 1940's as it was discovered that it was used as a place to hide secret weapons during World War 2. There were records containing the exact reason why Lenton's Cross was not reopened to the public after the war, but a fire in the mid 1950's burnt all records for the station and so, the station today remains a mystery. All trains stopped going to that station and a new one was built instead. But in recent days, a few eyewitness reports have stated that a vintage train has been seen leaving the station, suggesting trespassing of some sort,' the news reporter explained.

I fidgeted on my seat and watched intently. *Could this be related to the news article I read earlier? How would a train enter an abandoned station? None of this makes any sense.* I continued to watch the news in the hope that some of my questions would be answered. As I looked up, I was captivated by the eyewitness being interviewed.

'I don't know what happened really. I was sitting drinking coffee with my friend at my house, and we went on a walk. We walked past Lenton's Cross, and I turned my back for a second and then she was gone. I haven't heard from her since,' the young woman said, trying to hold back obvious tears.

'That is very strange. And you didn't see or hear anything?' The news reporter asked her, shoving the microphone in her face.

'No, nothing. It is all such a blur. The police have been looking for her ever since I reported her missing. Her parents are so worried,' she explained.

I turned the television off. So many bad things were happening in the world, even locally. I didn't even know there was an abandoned train station around here, how creepy! I couldn't even cope with going to a functioning train station. I couldn't imagine anything quite like it.

NOW

This whole time, Mary knew more than anyone else on this train. She knew what we were up against and sat back whilst we suffered. What kind of woman could do that?

'Well? Explain yourself,' I insisted.

A look of worry carried itself over Mary's face. I saw it in her eyes, inescapable fear. *Was she just as terrified as me?*

'It wasn't always this way. We used to be a normal family, but these things happen once power goes to your head. I try to ask him about things, but he just says it's to remain a mystery,' Mary told me.

A recent memory began to rack my brain. Someone acting suspicious and saying they want to remain a mystery. What a coincidence! But what if it wasn't a coincidence? Who was it? The man at the train station! It was all coming back to me. Did he have something to do with this?

'Wait. That sounds awfully familiar. I met a man at my local train station a few days ago. He started talking to me about trains and hinted that he knew something about some missing people. Is that who you are talking about here? You better explain yourself Mary!' I bellowed. Stephen glared at us both back and forth, deliberately avoiding getting involved in the conversation. He was a nervous wreck that hated trouble by the look of things.

'This is just the beginning. He has much bigger plans. He said I join him, or he'll kill me too. You have to understand, I never meant for any of this to happen. I didn't want it to go like this!' Mary said as I watched what I hoped were genuine tears trickle down her wrinkled cheeks.

How could I feel sorry for her? She was letting innocent people be harmed and killed just to save her own skin. How could I trust her? If she knew what this guy was doing, did she even try to stop him? Maybe she would do anything to protect him.

'Who is this guy to you and why do you feel the need to protect him?' I asked.

'He's my son. I had him when I was 14 and he's ruined my life ever since. Everything that has happened on this train, he's planned meticulously. It's all he's thought about for 10 years,' she finally said.

'Why not go to the police? Tell them that your son is killing random people on a train?' I questioned.

'Because it wouldn't work! They would see me as an old, hysterical woman. They would never believe the things he has already done, not without solid evidence. He's been very good at covering his tracks. If he knew the police were onto him, he would just do it all earlier and kill me in the process for betraying him. You don't know what he's really like. The past 10 years have been all about surviving for me. Doing what he says so I can live to see another day. But there's something about you, something special. I have a feeling you won't fall victim to him, not like the others,' she went on, almost forgetting to take a breath in between words.

'So, you're saying these sick mind games he's playing on this train cannot be won? Do I have a chance at surviving this?' Stephen interjected; his hands visibly quivering.

Mary flashed him a look of sympathy and shame. I looked anywhere to avoid Stephen's eyes; I knew exactly what Mary was saying. If I had little chance of surviving and I was "special" then Stephen had no chance. He was just a nobody to Mary's son. Another young life sacrifice like it was nothing.

'No answer. That's a definite no survival then, right? Fuck it. The thing that makes all of this even harder for me is the waiting. Waiting to die, waiting for someone else to kill me. I almost killed myself once when my own father abused me, maybe I should just do it now. It's my time to go anyway, why let some crazy stranger do it?' Stephen went on. He had lost a sense of himself that could never be returned. He had accepted death.

Before we had the chance to reply, he scurried over to the lasers. Sharing my knowledge of the lasers would kill him, deep feelings of shame and regret floated around my body. Could I not save anyone? Was it even my job to save people?

'Now come on. We can beat this! Mary here will get us out alive, right?' I raised my eyebrows at Mary, hoping she would back me up and give him something to keep going for. She chose to say nothing instead, she chose not to give a young man hope at the worst time of his life. *Who was I dealing with here?* Maybe my words weren't powerful enough to give him something to live for.

'It's okay, I know this is my time to die. I've accepted it. There's nothing anyone can do. I just can't wait around for it to happen; I need to regain control. But I won't die by lasers, not like some low budget horror film. No. I'll die my way,' Stephen explained.

My heart broke for him but who was I to stop him? I could save people that wanted to live but I had no chance of saving someone who was ready to go. He had no fight left in him and I was a stranger to him. He wouldn't listen to me; this was a battle that I just couldn't win. How would he do it? Would we be forced to watch? Panic crept up on me, stealing my senses and attacking my nerves. Death was always hard, but this would surely be more difficult to witness.

He walked away from the lasers, and I noticed the hostages looked just as nervous as me. He paced a small section of the train repeatedly. Did he know what he was going to do? Had he been planning it for hours? He walked into the driver's compartment and locked the door. *Maybe he didn't want us to see him end his life.* I looked away but Mary watched. She winced but she didn't turn away. What did he have in there that could kill him? It was then that we heard a loud thud, it was over for him. Mary jolted over to the driver's cabin and pulled the door open.

'Nobody come in here. He's gone. Looks like it was quick. He must have been smart, he electrocuted himself with the right voltage to kill him straight away. Such a shame he had to go like that,' Mary stated.

I chose not to ask questions, his life was over and as devastating as it was, we couldn't afford to waste any more time on it. I watched Mary walk back over to me, the hostages staring her out as she walked past them.

'So? How does he do it? How did he kill me a couple of times and bring me back to life? This whole time I thought I was going crazy! What is all this? Some sort of experiment on a vintage train? Will Stephen come back to life next? Whatever it is, he needs to be stopped!' I yelled, my voice box shaking with fear and the words stumbling out of my mouth clumsily.

'Bring you back to life? What? No, he doesn't have powers! He's using this train and everyone on it to see who the chosen one is, to test humanity before his big finale. Wait. You actually believe you've been resurrected? Maybe you are crazy too!' Mary shouted back to me. Our voices were now overpowering the sound of the train against the tracks.

'No, I'm serious! Jonas, he killed me. He threw me over the sacrifice line before we figured out how to survive round one. But then I woke up, I was reborn. I got another chance and I survived it! It almost feels like something is watching over me, making sure I survive no matter what. It's impossible I know but it happened! I have memories as clear as day. And you, you killed me with the lasers, but I woke up again. That's how I knew about the switch!' I explained.

I felt my forehead dripping with cold sweat. I felt the hostages' heads switch from mine to Mary's, trying to take in everything we were saying. They must have been terrified, the more we talked, the more time we lost to rescue them.

'How did you know what I was going to do! No, no this cannot be right. Unless. Unless you really are the chosen one. The one my son is so afraid of,' she suggested.

'The chosen one? What do you mean?' I asked.

She looked at me as though she was staring into my soul before she said, 'the chosen one. The chosen one I have been seeing in my dreams all these years. The one that will stop all this from happening and save us all. The one that must survive.'

Chapter 8

1946

'What was it that they were saying about this place? Bad things keep happening or something? Everyone's gone a bit mad since the end of the war. They've got nothing better to do,' a mature dark-haired man named John told his friend, in a stern voice.

'I heard there were a few dead broads. But there's all sorts of rumours going around. Anyway, I ain't here to have a nice chat. Let's just block this station off and get home. My wife has an egg and sausage pie waiting for me. So, I can...Jesus Christ!

Step back, step back!' Carlos, a young muscular gentleman called out.

'Yeah yeah Carlos. Nice try. I know ghosts don't exist; I have God's word on that one. Try and trick somebody else, yeah?' John giggled.

'I mean it! These things could still be live! They look like chemical bombs, that poisonous stuff! We need to call the bomb squad down here, section it off and let's get out of here now!' Carlos yelled. His voice echoed down the eerie empty tunnels.

John looked around and realised that his eyes couldn't disagree with his friend's claim. There were a couple of mini chemical bombs just lying there near the tracks. Lenton's Cross was unsafe for the public, for anyone. It seemed that it had been a secret storage place for weapons during the war that nobody had since discovered. The men wondered if there were also more dangerous bombs underground, right under their feet. Carlos and John sectioned the whole station off and jogged outside to safety. They locked up the station, never to be uncovered again. Not for many years to come.

NOW

    I ingested her words as though my body was a starving vessel finally being fed after weeks of suffering. Was this the answer I had been waiting for? What did being "the chosen one" really mean? Could I even believe Mary? I couldn't do anything until the hostages had been saved. I looked up at the timer and time was running out. I remembered that we had already discussed the laser switch a while ago, but I was so caught up in our conversation that I forgot to press it. For the first time in my life, I felt selfish for wanting to get answers to my questions instead of helping those poor people.

'What are you talking about? Please, save the hostages before we talk, we can't risk the timer going off,' I said nervously.

She rolled her eyes and pressed the green button, turning the lasers off. I dashed over to the hostages and pulled the tape from their mouths and untied them. They said thank you and began to talk amongst themselves. The timer stopped and I jogged back over to Mary to continue our conversation. I honestly believed these mind games would be more difficult, but I guess I wouldn't have figured it out so quickly if Mary didn't kill me first. I had an advantage over everyone by coming back to life, it meant I knew how to figure the mind games out quicker, and I didn't have to worry about dying for good.

'For years it has been happening. I had nightmares about the impact my son would have on the world if he got his own wicked way. But then I let it slip that I was having vivid dreams showing certain people I'd never even met before. He used my descriptions to kidnap certain people, nobody on these trains were picked at random. But in these dreams, when things seemed doomed, someone stopped it all from happening. They saved us all. I never saw their face, just a figure in the distance with a light around them. I never imagined I would get to meet them before my son did. I have no idea how all this is supposed to end, I just know you are the key to the whole world surviving. He despised the fact that someone was supposed to stop him, so he said I'd know when I met everyone who it was, and he was right. I just knew when I saw you.' Mary went on.

    I couldn't tell whether things were finally making sense and falling into place, or I was even more confused than before. My mind automatically took me back to the flyer that hit my kitchen window, the one that said I had been chosen. Was that some sort of sign? I felt I had no choice but to believe Mary, who else did I have? There was no way off this train, nowhere to turn but the unknown. Why would she lie? What could she gain from lying? Nothing. I *had* to believe her.

'I'm the key to the whole world surviving? But how? And why me? There are plenty of more capable people in this world than me. Surely this is some mistake? I have an unusual fear of trains, I always have. And you're telling me that someone who is scared of trains can save the world? No, this has to be wrong.'

I tried to convince her that I wasn't capable but maybe I was trying to convince myself. *Did any of us truly know ourselves? Did I really know what I was capable of?* Perhaps Mary saw something in me that I didn't. There was nothing worse than the pressure of saving lives, especially the whole world.

'You must believe it, there is no other option. Once this train does its final lap, we are all doomed, not just the people on this train. It will set the final stage of the plan in motion. Do you know where we are right now?' Mary asked.

When I really thought about it, no I didn't. I had no idea at all where this train currently was. The whole thing was too daunting to comprehend. The map that I found didn't even make sense. I feared that if I even tried to think about where I currently was or where I was heading, I would have a complete meltdown and lose all my senses. It would all seem too real and the realisation that I could die for real would take over a little too much. I'd be no use to anyone. I needed full concentration today of all days, I had to keep composure at all times. I gently shook my head to confirm that I had no idea where we were, and I was ready for her to enlighten me.

'I didn't think so. We are currently in the dark tunnels of Lenton's Cross station,' she told me. I felt my jaw slightly drop as she spoke.

'Lenton's Cross? As in the abandoned station that has been untouched since just after the war? But how? It's been blocked off from all public use,' I enquired.

'My son, he makes the impossible tasks seem easy. And there's no way to stop him once he gets an idea into his head. This is his final experimental train; we don't have long to figure something out to stop him! As I said before, it all started 10 years ago. I tried to talk sense into him, but he wouldn't listen...'

10 YEARS AGO

'Yes, this is perfect! A lot of research has gone into this. This is the place where all my dreams will be carried out. As dangerous as ever, I love it. Just don't touch anything, they're all still live. I don't want them to be damaged,' he sniggered.

'Look, Anthony my darling. Don't you think it's time to move on from all this? You've been dwelling on this place for months and it's not healthy. Not just that, think of all the things that could go wrong. The police could find out what you're doing in here, someone walking past could hear you working down here. It's just too risky,' Mary answered.

'Silence. I don't want this speech all over again. I know you don't agree with me mother, but that won't stop me from reaching big. Just think of how amazing it will be, you and I would be the only survivors left, and the workers of course if they do as I ask. The whole world to ourselves. We could take whatever we wanted, the only dictator in history to possess the world!' Anthony continued. Mary winced at the sight of greed in her son's eyes. She wondered how such a well-mannered and intelligent young man had grown to be so malicious.

'I have wanted expensive gowns and jewels all my life, but this is wrong. We can't all get what we want! This is a disaster on a large scale! I can't let you kill all these people just to satisfy your own goals, no I won't let you. Do not build that safety tunnel under this station, we have no right to survive above everyone else. I need to tell someone about what you're doing.'

Mary tried to reason with him, she wished with every bone in her body that he would see sense and change his devious plans. Anthony's face didn't alter, no sympathy reflected in his eyes. He took pleasure in laughing in her face.

'Oh mother. What will you do? You're nothing but a miserable old woman and you will do as I say. We all have our roles to play in this. Now, better get started,' Anthony said with a smirk tugging at the corners of his mouth.

Mary was viciously pushed aside as the work men that were hired by Anthony began their work. Mary gazed over at her son with disappointment. How could he do this? How had her son grown to be so selfish and vindictive? She worried for the whole world; she knew what he was capable of. It occurred to her that the only one who could save everyone was someone from her dreams. Were they even real?

NOW

'Wait. So, what you are saying is your son found the chemical bombs and then dug up Lenton's Cross to build a safety tunnel for him to hide out in? How would that end the world? It would probably spread across half the city, but that's all,' I said once she had finished telling me the story.

Mary clenched her fist tightly. Fear and frustration created the perfect pool of emotion in her eyes. I could see her pain; I *felt* her pain. She was a mother. Something I had never been, something I could never be. A mother that would do anything to protect her son but not at the expense of others. It was killing her to share this information, but she trusted me enough to do so. *Surely that meant something?*

'It's chemical warfare that most people are aware of, they're poisonous and extremely dangerous. Europe never used them during the Second World War, but they had them on standby in case they needed them. They were found in Lenton's Cross a few years after the war and that's when the station was sectioned off to the public. They stored thousands of them, enough to cause a global impact. Over these 10 years since he found the bombs, he has hired people to go to every single city in the world and secretly plant two of the bombs at either side. He has a detonator for every single one of them. He is a perfectionist and he's left no stone unturned; everything is planned down to the last second with him,' she paused, lifting her eye contact from me and suddenly looking all over the place.

'He has named it the "Anthon Affect" and hopes it will go down in history, if humans don't go extinct eventually that is. They are guaranteed to wipe out at least 80% of the population within 20 minutes. I don't have long left anyway but I won't be able to go peacefully knowing that my offspring will ruin the whole planet. This is not how I want things to end. The thought of people being poisoned to death, having no warning and then the atmosphere of the planet being ruined, it's too much to bear,' Mary explained.

A tear fell from her glittering eyes. I could see it now. Her weak, feeble bones. Her pale, oily skin.

She was living out her final days and doing what she could to save everyone before she gave into death. *How could her own son put her through this? He had to be stopped. But how?* How could I stop his powerful bombs from going off when I finally faced him?

'I am sorry. I didn't realise. Everyone deserves to go peacefully, not like this. Not with the weight of the world on their conscience. But how? Tell me how I could possibly stop your son from killing the whole planet? You already said these chemical weapons are already planted in every city. We could try telling someone of authority what he is up to but why would they believe us? I am just a woman, like you. There is nothing special about me, there never has been,' I told her.

As I spoke and indirectly demanded more answers, my eyes were suddenly drawn to the tape that the hostages had across their mouths before we rescued them. They were scattered unevenly across the floor. I felt myself edging closer to them, once again having no control of the movements of my legs.

My hand reached for three of them. I turned them over and words were carved into them. *There was definitely no writing on the tape before. Is this a sign?* I stared closely to read them. They said: "Purity", "Courage" and "Kindness". I put my hand out to Mary so she could see them.

'You can see that, right? Writing has appeared on this tape,' I said with my hand shaking slightly.

She took the tape from my hand and examined them, turning them in all directions. She awkwardly shook her head and handed them back to me.

'I don't see anything, but I believe you. In the dreams I had, there was a voice in the background that said the one who sees the signs is the key. Maybe this is what it means. What do the words on the tape say?' Mary explained to me.

'It says purity, courage and kindness, straight after I asked why me. I guess someone answered my question for me. Someone must see potential in me that I can't see within myself. Someone or something. How long until we reach our destination?' I asked.

'There are many more rounds yet. If you really are the key to ending all this, the one from my dreams, we need to figure out how to do this quickly. Which means I need to make sure we get to the destination early before any more rounds can be played. Betraying him is a big risk for me but I couldn't live with myself if I didn't help you to do the right thing. It's time to face him, even if it means I die trying.'

Chapter 9

I stared down at my palms, was this real? Had I really come this far just for this ending? I let the blood trickle through my fingers and splatter on the ground. He looked over at me, smirking. The guilt flooded inside me; I could not live like this. The ground beneath me began to shake, small cracks started to appear in the station's ceiling. *What was happening?* The abandoned station suddenly seemed even more unstable than before.

'What is this? What have you done!' His voice grated on my ear drums and made my skin crawl with anger, but I didn't answer him. I looked up at the gold-plated station clock on the wall, it was turning 6am.

I crawled back over to her lifeless body, bending down to check her pulse once again. No, she had definitely gone. *Was it my fault?* How would I explain this? He needed to be punished. I looked over at the train that my worst nightmare took place on. I shouldn't have spent years fearing trains, I should have feared what could happen on them instead.

Everything was a blur; I couldn't think straight. It felt like the end, *was it the end?* I had made a terrible mistake; we were all doomed. A greater power trusted me to end this, and I failed, I screwed up. He came over to me, shaking his head. I noticed a tiny mark of graffiti on a wall behind him, it read "you are alone, it's over".

'I knew you would do as I say, you fool,' he echoed in my ear, hovering over me dominantly. He took hold of my shoulder, forcefully shoving the knife in and out of my body. I tried to see the intense pain as a punishment, but I soon lost count of how many times he stabbed me. I tried not to panic, hoping I would once again be reborn. As I struggled for breath,

I laid there in my own blood. He backed off, wiping his face and discarding the knife onto the tracks. I couldn't keep my eyes open, I squirmed at the feeling of the blood pouring out of my wounds. This wasn't right. Maybe I shouldn't have done what he asked, perhaps I made a mistake that I could never come back from. This time, dying felt strange, it felt *final*.

***

'Charlene? Did you hear what I said?' Mary's loud voice shocked me back into the here and now.

'Sorry, what?' I said, looking around to get my bearings. *I was still on the train.*

'You were staring into space for a good minute or so. Are you okay?' She asked.

She had been honest with me so far; it was only right that I did the same. After all, what did I have to lose?

'It felt so real. It's the first time I've ever had a dream while awake. Weird. Anyway, let's get on with what we were talking about,' I shrugged it off.

'A dream while you were awake? That is a vision. It could tell you what is going to happen next or maybe even warn you what not to do. Anyway, I said it's time we face him even if he harms me,' Mary answered.

The more I tried to think of the dream or vision I had, the more the details disintegrated into the deep depths of my mind. Nothing so far had been a mere coincidence; everything had a purpose. But what good would it do if I couldn't remember most of it?

'But how? I get the feeling we cannot choose when we face him, the rounds have to play out first,' I replied.

She shook her head and wafted her finger in the air as though she was thinking of every possible scenario.

'There is always a way. The original plan was that I would go on this train with the experimental passengers and try to figure out which person it was that I saw in my dream. The minute I was sure, I was supposed to make sure they died to eliminate any threats to the big finale. But I know how many loops of the station this train is supposed to do and I'm pretty sure I can use that to catch him off guard.' Mary explained thoroughly.

'Well, I guess that explains why you killed me with the lasers and didn't tell me anything about the rounds. I guess he wasn't expecting me to come back to life whenever I was killed, it's been a shock for me too. It's unexplainable. But he is your son. How do I know you won't back out and take his side the minute we get there?' I suggested. I began to pace the length of the train as I spoke; the feeling of fear rising with each word.

'I know this isn't very reassuring right now but all I can say is you will have to trust me,' she said.

She walked past me to the train cab. She reached into her pocket and took out a key to get into it. I sighed, the realisation that this whole thing had been fixed so that I'd die started sinking in. The thought of all those poor souls that died on this train over an old lady's dreams. It was devastating. But someone wanted me to live. *Or something.* Would I ever find out who was looking out for me? Bringing me back to life but nobody else? My heart ached at the thought of never getting any answers. No time to think or get answers, just to survive. I followed her into the cab and hovered over her shoulder as she began to press the controls. I looked behind me and saw the other passengers sitting down and chatting.

'Just give me a few minutes, I'm a little rusty. I operated trains for a while when I was in my 30's. I've dabbled in different jobs, it will just take a bit of time,' she told me.

Was there anything else I would find out about this woman? Her son was a maniac, she was terminally ill and now, she could drive trains. I sighed with shock and walked out towards the rescued hostages. A calmness suddenly came over me unexpectedly. The possibility of me dying on this train was shrinking by the second. Now that I had my bearings and Mary and I had an understanding, maybe the worst was over.

'We heard what you were saying back there. Did you say you kept dying and coming back to life?' A timid voice called out to me. I stepped back to face them all, ensuring they could all hear my response.

'It would appear that way, yes. I know it sounds crazy and I don't have an explanation right now but that is what happened. I am still alive even though I know what it's like to die,' I responded with my head hanging low.

'I've heard about this sort of thing, a time loop. The type where you are only dead for a few seconds and then you are reborn, and you have to live that same moment again until it goes differently. You hear about these things, don't you? They say fate doesn't let anyone die if they have a purpose to serve. Maybe that's what is happening here?' He replied to me.

'Yeah! That is exactly what it felt like. It almost felt like a greater power couldn't let me die, they wanted me to succeed. For the first time in my life, I felt like I had a purpose, like petty fears meant nothing because I was needed for something greater than myself. It's all so unclear to me still but I know what I need to do now. I need to stop a man from detonating bombs that will ruin the planet...' My speech was cut short when an old looking man interrupted me.

'Oh, come on. She's insane! Do not listen to her. There's no way she kept coming back from the dead, that's impossible. Stop swallowing her bullshit! Yeah, she saved us and I'm grateful, but I don't believe in all that crap. It's just some sick guy's way of making his own entertainment, that's all,' the man said. The two men began to have a heated argument when Mary came to the doorway of the cab and waved me through.

'I have sped up the train. I've also disabled the timers for all of the rounds. I won't let any more rounds take place, I just can't. I will have to take my son's wrath when I see him, which should be very soon,' Mary explained.

I felt grateful for her sudden loyalty. But there were still doubts swimming around my mind. *Could I really trust her? Was she still on his side? Would she betray me? What if I died permanently?* The sad truth was that I had no other choice; I had to take a risk and follow her lead.

'Okay, thank you. Wait. Won't there be cameras or something that are monitoring the rounds? It will put our whole plan at risk if he knows we are getting to him early.' I asked, my voice jittering as I tried to force my words out.

'No, he trusted me to keep mental notes of who won what round, who died and the rest. He thinks I have nothing to lose with me already being on death's door but he's wrong. Don't worry, we have full control from this point on,' Mary attempted to reassure me. 'We won't be far now, just a few minutes away. We've been doing loops around Lenton's Cross this whole time. It starts and ends in the same station. He won't see us coming, we have the advantage,' she went on.

I stared out of the window, letting my mind wonder. I focused on the constant nothingness rushing by, it felt similar to my experience on the underground when I was a teenager. My focus was broken when my eyes forced me to hold my gaze on the emergency stop lever. I disregarded it and continued to casually look around the train, but my eyes continued to hover over the lever.

Something urged me to pull it down, to force the train to stop. *But why? And why now?* We were on the way to confront Mary's son, we were nearing the end of this nightmare, but my body wanted me to stop the train? It made me question whether it was a sign or my irrational fear of trains making me panic. Before

I had the chance to think, the train began to unsteadily shake.

A loud screech clouded my thoughts and suffocated my eardrums. It suddenly felt as though we were on a rickety fairground ride, our bones shaking uncontrollably as though our flesh could drop off them at any second. Some of the rescued passengers were thrown from their seats, their faces were aggressively pressed against the windows. Gravity threw Mary and I into one another, our shoulders smashing together. The force caused us to fall in the opposite directions.

'No, he's taken control of the train, how did he know!' Mary bellowed, her voice barely audible above the cries of bending metal.

I launched forward, keeping the emergency lever in my sights. *It must have been a sign, it's a risk but I need to pull it now.* I dived towards it, managing to just grab it before the train threw me off balance again. He must have somehow known we had messed with the controls on the train and tried to scare us or even kill us by causing a train crash. He was willing to do anything to make sure we all died on this train. I successfully pulled the lever down before violently crashing on the ground below it. After a few aggressive shudders, the train came to a halt. I heard the uneven breathing of each passenger, silently thanking me for saving them once again. Their eyes became flooded with relief as I managed to bring the train to a halt.

'The emergency lever, of course! I didn't even think that thing would still work,' Mary sighed, trying to get her breath back.

'I think it was a sign, someone is still on our side. What now? He just controlled the train and nearly killed us so he must still be watching us somehow,' I questioned, hoping Mary would have a better idea of what was going on than I did.

'I think it's time for the chosen one to rest,' one of the passengers whispered behind me.

I felt a hard knock to the back of my skull. I tried to keep my balance, but my limbs turned bitterly weak, and I face planted the floor at full pelt. My eyes wanted to shut but I resisted for a few painful seconds until I lost the fight. Everything around me went fuzzy and then, there was nothing.

SEVERAL MOMENTS LATER

When my eyes finally came into focus, my mind didn't cooperate. Nothing around me was registering and my memory wasn't great at first. I couldn't think about what had happened or where I was, it was all too much. But noticing someone standing over me and talking forced me to gather my bearings.

'I suppose you are pleased with yourself? You truly believe yourself to be some sort of hero, the chosen one. Protector of the people,' he chuckled to himself 'Ha! I planned everything, everything! Did you really think I would let someone ruin my plans this close to the end? I didn't expect the chosen one to be so naive!' He cackled.

I clumsily rose to my feet, one hand resting on the back of my head to feel the damage. And then it hit me. *Someone on that train harmed me.* The moment I looked him in the eyes, I knew it was him. The same guy from the train station, Mary's son. *Wait. Where was Mary?* I looked around me but there was just me and him. We were on a train platform, presumably in the same station. *How long was I out for? What did he gain from me being knocked out?* Before I even had the chance to consider replying to him, he filled the air with his voice once more.

'I do not believe that someone can be that pure. My mother sees you as some sort of saint, but we all have some bad in us, right?' He went on.

Was he playing mind games with me? Then I noticed it. A detonator hanging out of his trouser pocket. It finally dawned on me that there was only me between him and the whole world being in severe danger. Everything Mary had told me appeared to be true. There was no way out of this, I either stopped him or I died along with everyone else on the planet. I had come this far; I was not about to give up when it mattered the most.

'Who betrayed me? Who pretended to be on my side and then attacked me on the train like that?' I asked, not understanding why I bothered as he was bound to lie.

'Oh, she speaks!' He laughed at his own joke. 'I told you I had thought of every possible angle, I'm not stupid. My mother had done nothing but express her disappointment in me lately, there was no way I trusted her. I knew she would betray me and hope you would win, that's why I placed a trusted worker as a hostage to put things right if they went south.' He smirked as he spoke, his mouth tilting to one side.

'So, you had someone undercover this whole time? Where is Mary? What have you done with her!' I exclaimed. I tried to sound authoritative, but it was nothing more than a frightened squeak. 'She was afraid you would punish her for going against you and you have, haven't you!'

'Enough talking, it's time for the ritual. You need to show me and whatever is keeping you alive that you are not a good person! Once that is done, you will no longer be protected. You can be disposed of, and the final phase of my plan can finally go ahead!' He aggressively answered.

Ritual? What was he talking about? Whatever it was, I had a knot in my stomach that felt worse than just before I died. Surely, he couldn't put me through anything worse than what happened on the train. I finally let a thought cross my mind, one I had been trying to push away throughout this nightmare. *My family. Did they know I was still alive? Was I now a missing person too?* No matter what happened next, I needed to make it home. I had to find a way to expose his plans and save the whole planet. It was apparently my fate to do so. My thoughts were brought to a sudden halt when he aggressively dragged Mary out from behind a wall. She was gagged, her hands tied just like the hostages. *He was a monster. How could he do this to his own mother?*

'No, no! You cannot hurt her! Just let her go, end this madness once and for all. You don't need to hurt her!' I pleaded as I tried to force my eyes to hold my tears but failed.

'Oh, I won't be doing anything to hurt my mother. You will.'

Chapter 10

6 MONTHS AGO

A bus felt calmer than a train anyway. I could sit comfortably gazing out of the window, watching different coloured cars whooshing past. They weren't smooth runners like trains, but they felt safer to me. One more stop to go. I waited patiently as the bus kept stopping and starting at nearly every stop. I was in a bit of a rush, but not enough to panic over. It was only a weekly food shop. The bus came to a halt and an ageing gentleman stood beside my seat, struggling to walk to the opening bus doors. I immediately rose to my feet and began to assist him.

'Thank you, young lady. It is nice to see a pleasant person for a change,' he said, his warm eyes soaking up my welcoming smile.

'You are very welcome, sir,' I answered.

His clothes were nothing but tatters, frayed at the edges. Stained, the material visibly wearing out. He looked as though he hadn't eaten in days. Why did such kind people have to suffer? I dipped into my back pocket, gripping the last 30 I had until I got paid, the money for my food shop. I quickly dropped it behind him when he was concentrating on wobbling to the doors. I bent down, grasping it back into my palm.

'Sir, wait. You dropped this!' I held out my palm, offering him the money and hoping he would accept it as a kind gesture.

'Money? But I—' His talking stopped when his eyes met mine. I allowed the generosity to flood through me and reflect into his soul.

'Thank you, I will never forget this,' he took the money and placed it under his worn cap. You ever heard that old wife's tale? Do good for 24 hours and fate will do the hard part? Only 23 hours of good deeds to go!'

'What does that even mean?' I sniggered, amused by the wise old man before me.

'They say it's something to do with fate rewarding you if you make constant good decisions. See you around and thanks again,' he saluted me as he got off the bus, I politely waved as the bus continued on its journey.

NOW

I couldn't harm her or anyone, I just couldn't. I had spent the whole time on that trap riddled train only thinking of others. I didn't have a violent bone in my body. *Why did he think harming Mary would get rid of me? Did he know more than I did?*

He pressed his hand into the back of her neck and slammed her down before me. She was there, on her knees staring directly into my soul. There was no look of desperation as I pictured, she was more prepared for this outcome than I ever would be. Could I really kill someone? A stranger? Especially after trying so hard to save lives on that train. He closed his eyes and pressed his hands together, *was he praying?*

'Dear universe of fate, wherever you are. I present to you a woman, but she is just a woman. She was not born to be a hero; she has evil in her as do I and all humans. You see a purity in her that does not exist. My great destruction of the world will reset everything; it will give you full control once I have lived my life. Humans have ruined this planet for centuries, destroyed everything good. I will stop that, I'll stop it all,' he stared at the ceiling of the station while speaking. He clearly believed he was talking to something greater than humanity. 'I will now show you who this woman really is, why she doesn't deserve to live above all others. Above me! Then you can punish her, show her she is nothing special and finally let me have my way! You'll see that she can also commit vile sins and bring chaos and harm, just as I have,' It was then that I saw it, a carving knife hanging from his coat pocket.

He really did want me to kill his mother, to show the universe that I wasn't as pure as it thinks I am. Even if there was any truth to his method of madness, would there be a way to prove it? If he killed me, would I just come back to life again? *Maybe I had to just let him kill me and hope I would come back to life again and try something new. I would beat this, I had to.* He reached down, placing the knife into my palms and aggressively squeezing my fingers, involuntarily tightening my grip around it.

'Do it, end her,' he said coldly.

I felt I had no choice; I was terrified of him and the things he had already done for 10 years. Mary knew that this would happen, she had prepared herself for it. I never got the opportunity to prepare myself for this when I woke up this morning. There was no sign of fear anywhere on her face.

'No, I won't. What will you do if I don't?' I asked, wanting to know exactly where I stood before I did anything else. *Why would I be afraid of death when I had already died before?* I felt invincible. A greater power was on my side, and it would protect me, wouldn't it?

'I have intel on you. Where you live, your family, your friends. If you don't kill my mother right now, I will get my associates to go and murder your family. Just before they die, I will make sure they know who got them killed. If you do as I say, I may just have enough room in my tunnel for you and your family. All you have to do is prove you have evil in you, punish her for betraying me and then join me,' he explained.

Could I trust him? Did he really know my family? The thought of my immediate family being murdered in cold blood and the last word they ever heard was my name, almost stopped my heart. If I let him kill them, I would have done all of this for nothing. I had never just been fighting for my own life, but for my family and friends. Surviving to stop him meant I would save them. *Would I be able to live with myself knowing I had killed an innocent old lady just to save my family? Would her ghost forever haunt me? Was it a mercy killing if she was already dying?*

All of the possible outcomes and questions raced through my mind like trains crashing into one another at full speed. I closed my eyes for a second and took a deep breath, recalling what I had been through on that train. I always found a way out somehow but what if this really was it? I winced in pain as I realised, I had been pressing my palm into the razor-sharp blade. I peered down at the blood trickling tenderly down the middle of my palm.

Blood. My mind was viciously dragged back to the vision I had on the train. I couldn't remember it at the time, but the sight of blood brought it all back. *I remembered everything.* I was staring at Mary's blood on my hands, her body was still next to me. He didn't keep his promise, he stabbed me and watched me die. As the vivid memories of the visions returned, that same feeling came back to me. That *final* feeling. Maybe the vision was a warning, telling me not to go ahead with the killing. To still do the right thing no matter what. Maybe it was always about putting everyone else before myself, about being a good person.

'You are testing my patience! Do it now!' He yelled.

Mary squinted her eyes and looked away, she believed I had to do it too. *But I didn't.* I let the knife glide through my fresh blood and waited for it to clatter on the ground.

'No, I am not doing this. I am sticking with my morals. Killing is wrong, everything you are doing is wrong. I will never join you, no matter what it costs me!' I passionately called out. Mary opened her eyes; a slight smile began to form on her face. She looked almost proud of my words.

'It will cost you your family! How can you be such a "saint" if you would rather them die than kill my mother!' His face scrunched up as he spoke, his eyes turning a darker shade. I had never seen someone so full of hate before.

I had kept to my principles but what if he was right? Just because I refused to kill Mary, it didn't mean I was in the clear. I had put my family in danger instead. Was this really the right call? A tremendous amount of doubt entered my body, shifting my whole being and making me incredibly nauseous. *What could I do now?*

My vision showed a different path, I had no idea where this path of righteousness would take me. Just as I was struggling to think of a way out of this mess and save my family, a crack of light appeared in the ceiling of the station. Mary and I stared up at it, forcing Anthony to turn around to see what we were giving our attention to.

'What is this? Have you told someone what is happening here! How?' He cried.

Before I had the chance to reply or think, the light became immense. It almost blinded me. It came through tiny cracks on the station walls at first, but it soon expanded and continued to grow. I was eventually forced to close my eyes when it became too illuminating. It felt as though I was being consumed by the sun. I kept my eyes shut, hoping whatever it was would be over soon. I opened my eyes when I felt the light shrinking.

***

I immediately began to observe my surroundings. This wasn't the station. The minute my eyes focused properly; I knew where I was. *I was at home.* I was sitting at the kitchen table. I jolted up as something hit the window, it was the flyer. *Wait, what is going on here? Why would a light take me back in time to live this nightmare again? I did everything it wanted me to!* I rushed to the window and closed it, making sure I didn't let the flyer in this time. I needed clarity. Maybe this was a second chance and none of it happened? Maybe fate reset it all?

I bolted into the living room and put the TV on. If everything was as it was the day I got on that train, the missing people would still be plastered all over the news. I flicked to the news channel, hoping for a miracle. I wanted the reassurance that everything I had gone through and always making the right decisions had led to me saving a planet full of people. I watched and listened. It was still happening.

The same people that went missing before me were still missing. So, what had I stopped? Why would a higher power help me just to achieve nothing? Had I got this whole thing wrong? Was it a sinister power at play here, not one that wanted people to live? But why would it make me survive?

The questions just wouldn't stop pouring into the forefront of my mind and leaking out into the unknown. *Wait. Anthony won't know that I'm not on the way to the train. He won't even be aware that I know all of his plans. I have time.* My body fell into an uncontrollable panic as I pushed myself towards the telephone. I dialled the police and began to chew the side of my nail impatiently. I continuously bobbed my leg up and down as I waited for them to answer. I was relieved to hear a voice at the other end of the phone.

'Hello, this is serious. Something needs to be done urgently! I know for a fact that someone is planning a terrorist attack on the whole world,' I blurted out.

'A terrorist attack? Is this a hoax ma'am? Or maybe you have taken some strong medication?' The officer replied.

'No, believe me this is real. He has been planting poisonous weapons in each city for 10 years. His action plan begins today, he needs to be stopped! He is the reason so many local people have been going missing, he has been eliminating anyone who may try to stop him, people in high paid jobs or the ones his mother sees in her dreams!' I explained. I tried to remain calm, but I must have sounded hysterical.

'That is a very serious accusation, ma'am. Please come to your local station to make a statement. We have a lot of these calls, and they turn out to be nothing. Do you know anyone else that could collaborate your story?' He asked. I immediately remembered how much Mary didn't agree with her son's actions. *Was it too much to think she would give him up? Maybe, but I didn't have any other option.*

'Yes. I don't know where she lives but perhaps you have her record? Her name is Mary. I don't know her surname, but she lives in this area. She is an old lady who has been diagnosed with a terminal illness,' I said. *Maybe that was too vague, I should have asked for more details!* I heard him sigh and begin to type in the background. I let the silence give me a moment to think, to catch my breath.

'There are only two Mary's living in this town. One is a 54-year-old woman who runs the community centre and the other is a 72-year-old widow. She has a son and is terminally ill,' he asserted.

'Yeah! That's her! It's her son that is doing all this!' I felt relief when he identified the correct woman, the only one that could back me up on this.

Not long later, I dashed down to the local station ready to give all the information I had in order to save everyone.

'Oh, are you the lady on the phone? The one reporting a terrorist attack of some sort?' He said, it was the same officer's voice I could tell.

'That's right. Something needs to be done or the whole world will suffer,' I blurted out as I began to breath heavily. It was probably easily noticed.

'Look, we have limited resources and I'm a new cop. I can't risk wasting my superior's time with this nonsense. Have you thought about getting checked into a psychiatric ward for an assessment or something? Shall I get a colleague that can help and—' he went on, but I had to interrupt him, I couldn't take hearing anymore of this.

'I'm sorry, no. That's not what this is. If you want proof, I can give you that. I can tell you the name of the man that has done this and exactly where he is now. All the evidence you need is at Lenton's Cross, and you need to get there fast if you want to save lives. Trust me or don't that's up to you. But it will be on you if the word gets out that people have died and you did nothing,' I sternly told him.

I heard the door of the station creak open a tad; I didn't bother to look around to see who had walked in. I had to focus on convincing the police that I wasn't some maniac trying to cause unnecessary panic.

'She isn't lying. I'm Mary, the one you called earlier. I can back up her story and give a statement. I have 10 year's worth of evidence because I hoped this day would come. The man you are looking for is my son,' a familiar and frail voice called from just behind me. I spun around on my ankles to face her.

'Mary? You came here and you're willing to turn your own son in just to back me up?' I cried with a grateful, teary look on my face.

'I know we've never met but you look familiar, the figure from my dreams. I know I can trust you just by meeting you. If it means they stop him in time, then yes, I'll tell them everything. And it will save the world, I have to do the right thing and leave this world in peace before I go,' Mary insisted.

The officer's face completely changed. He stopped glaring at me with sympathy and suspicion and began to look grateful. We were both taken into separate interview rooms where we gave full and truthful statements. I left the part out about how I kept dying and coming back to life in some sort of time loop because then I really wouldn't be doing myself any favours. I signed my name to the statement and hoped that this would be enough to have him arrested before his awful plans could go ahead. Surely, I didn't go through all of that death and misery for nothing, this had to be the end to it all.

I told him all about the abandoned train station and how he had somehow stole a pullman's train for his secret experiments and how it was where he planned to hide out when the chemical bombs were released. I let them know his motive – that he had a dream to be the only man left on the planet. I even explained my theory about how he had carefully picked his workers, men and women of a certain age that he would save in the tunnel too. Once everyone had been wiped out, he would be in charge of the new hierarchy, and he would be free to be a vicious dictator and do whatever he wanted.

He would probably even choose who each person had to be with in order to repopulate the planet on his terms. Once they had all the information they needed, they began to send armed police officers in riot gear towards the station. There was no way Anthony saw that coming.

I felt surprise run through my body as I didn't believe for a second that the police would take me seriously. If it wasn't for Mary, maybe they wouldn't have. It turned out that Anthony had an extensive criminal record that even Mary wasn't aware of, the police had every reason to believe our claims now.

Mary and I met up again just outside the station on our way out. I sensed her eyes on me, scanning me.

'There is one thing I don't get. You were supposed to be on that train, but you came here instead to tell the police. How did you know about his plans when nobody has told you yet? This doesn't make sense. I'm grateful that you knew and managed to stop him but how?' Mary questioned. I knew the questions were boiling beneath the surface the moment she saw me in the station.

'Let's just say fate gave me a helping hand. Don't worry Mary, your final days won't be lived in fear of your son. We've stopped him before it's too late.'

With my words, she hugged me tightly. The most sincere hug I had ever had. To help people felt amazing and I could live my life with the knowledge that I had saved everyone from that awful fate. *Maybe, it was finally over. And maybe I had just saved the lives of every single person on this planet, through nothing but human kindness.*

6 MONTHS LATER

I still had awful memories. What it felt like to die multiple times. Watching other people die, trying to figure out mind games before the timer ran out. Random clues appearing that nobody else could see. I got to walk around seeing people happy, knowing I saved them. It was true that nobody understood what I went through so they could live, but it was worth it. I didn't survive and save everyone just for the glory.

Anthony had been sentenced to many years in prison after most of his workers testified against him in court. I had regular coffee meet ups with Mary, she was growing weaker by the day unfortunately, but the doctors said it was unusual that she was still alive. This was it. I finally felt confident enough to board a train. I swore I'd never step on one ever again, especially after what happened to me, but my fears would consume me if I let them.

One good thing to come out of what I went through was the knowledge that I was brave, and I had a good heart. It helped me to tackle a lot of small fears and prove to myself that nothing could break me. I took my seat on the train and glared out of the window, trying to concentrate on anything but my anxieties. Anthony still had the odd person that was loyal to him, like the man that knocked me unconscious on the train, the undercover hostage.

He believed in Anthony's way of life and refused to testify against him, denying he saw anything. Nobody had seen him since Anthony was arrested. A man got on the train at the station after mine. He paced around as though he was looking for someone. He spotted me and stopped dead in his tracks before plonking himself down on the seat across from me. There were plenty of seats, but he chose to sit across from me. *Why?*

'Surely you didn't think you could get away with this, Charlene. Evil always wins,' a cold, deep voice said to me.

I looked up at the hooded man across from me. He removed his hood, and I felt the blood freeze in my veins. I even wondered if my blood could continue to pump after such an unexpected shock.

'You! How dare you speak to me after what you did! You could have done the right thing and stood up to him in court, but you bailed. How did you know what train I would be on?' I replied in a panicked voice. *How did he know where I'd be?*

'Someone had to stay loyal to him, he does have some decent friends. I'm no grass. I've been following you since you told the police about him. And now everything is in place, it's time,' he explained as he reached for his heavy looking rucksack. 'You see, some of Anthony's loyal friends and I have been working on a theory of our own. You've already saved everyone, Charlene. You no longer serve a purpose in this world and the only way to end this is through revenge. Your luck has run out, maybe you were supposed to die a hero on that train. Maybe you were always supposed to die. Well, your day has finally come,' his menacing voice echoed in my mind. *Was there any logical truth to his theory?*

Was that the plan all along? Was I supposed to figure all of this out about Anthony's big plans and save everyone but die anyway? Like a real sacrifice? Maybe it was the plan. Maybe I was always supposed to die on that train and for the past 6 months, I have been a ticking time bomb. How could fate be so cruel? I guess it's true what they said, some people are meant to die a hero. It really was my time, wasn't it? I wasn't prepared to die; I was prepared to start the rest of my life. But time wasn't on my side and this man didn't want to wait to end me. He reached into his bag and pulled out a shotgun.

I heard screams of fear from people on the train, but it didn't matter, nobody could save me now. I had no choice but to close my eyes and let the inevitable take over. I waited impatiently for the sound of the gun shot, the sound of the end. I knew how to die; I had done it many times. But the thought of never coming back shook me up more than the pain of death.

I had to accept that nobody could escape the inevitable. I would die angry. Angry at fate for putting me through that for nothing, angry at myself for not figuring out my ending sooner and angry that I would never be able to say goodbye to my family. I would be just another victim in a newspaper. Why? Why did this have to be me, right here and now? Surely this wasn't the end, *was it?*

Epilogue

SCARLET

It had been a few days since I emerged from Ridgebrooke. Going back to work seemed almost surreal. The pressure to act normal like a grieving daughter became overwhelming incredibly fast. It got me questioning everything. Was this really the life for me? It seemed that everything was slowly turning South since I returned, everything I heard on the news sounded worse than spending the rest of my life in a town that didn't appear on a map. Scientists were now speculating that the ozone layer was reaching its end and they had no idea how long it would be until it exploded.

I guess that was human kind's punishment for not taking climate change seriously. I knew Andrew would be terrified if he watched the news, he always researched things like that and scared himself half to death. That was if he was still alive. Maybe I'd never find out. I could only hope that if the Earth ever did blow up with no warning, I would be dead and buried already or Ridgebrooke would somehow survive the catastrophe and I would be sent there and survive. Who knows? I guess I may never find out. I had to focus on the now.

KALINA

It wasn't long until I had mastered being in spirit form. I had found a way to possess people, manipulate them to do what I wanted. All for the greater good of course. Until Josephine's baby was born, I used my ghostly ways to keep an eye on things. More people grieved for me than I thought they would, it brought me comfort. I couldn't speak to Kaiser; I didn't want to keep interfering with his new life.

He was giving his marriage a good go and I didn't want to ruin his happiness. He was doing amazingly well as the new leader. He had begun to expand further than Yalford Valley. He was working hard to discover why Yalford Valley was in a decent state compared to the rest of the world and I was proud of him. He had discovered an historic site from World War 2 which was over 1,000 years ago. Some train station that was used to store dangerous chemical bombs called Lenton's Cross. Who knew what else he might find down there?

CHARLENE

What? Where was I? He was definitely about to shoot me on that train so how was I still alive? Was fate still saving me? I scanned the area but all I could see were murky, misty skies and dark clouds. Ah, a sign! Ridgebrooke? I had never heard of the place! Wait. I remember the tale of Spencer and Lacey, the ones who claimed to be trapped in a mysterious town and somehow escaped. I'm sure they said it was called Ridgebrooke. I needed answers and I needed them now. But whatever I was about to face, it was surely better than death.

Printed in Great Britain
by Amazon